OTHER BOOKS

THEY CALL ME MAD DOG

FLAMING IGUANAS

Lap Dancing for Mommy

BY ERIKA ★ LOPEZ

HOOCHIE MAMA
LA OTRA CARNE BLANCA
simon & Schuster
by Mrs. Lopez

SiMON & SCHUSTER
Rockefeller Center
1230 AVENUE of the AMERICAS
New York, NY 10020

Simon & Schuster and COLOPHON are Registered trademarks of SIMON & SCHUSTER, Inc.

Designed by Erika Lopez [P.O. Box 410011/San Francisco, CA 94141 OR ErikaLopez.com]
"Bikini KAT" and "SMARt, sassy, stylish"-Trademarks of Kitty Katty's LLC/copyright owned by Flower Frankenste
Manufactured in the United States of America

10   9   8   7   6   5   4   3   2   1

Library of Congress Cataloging-in-Publication Data

Lopez, Erika.
Hoochie Mama : the other white meat / Erika Lopez.
     p. cm.
1. San Francisco (Calif.)—Fiction. 2. Women motorcyclists—Fiction.
3. Gentrification—Fiction. 4. Neighborhood—Fiction. I. Title.

PS3562.0672 H66 2001
813'.54—dc21   Library of Congress Control Number: 2001020282

ISBN 0-684-86974-8

Even though she'll never read this book,
I dedicate it to "Cherry" Mary Starvis,
to me, she is san francisco.

YOU MUST HEED THE CRY OF THE MUUMUU..
HOLD MY HAND ★ DON'T BE AFRAID.
YOU'RE SAFE FROM THE

LATTE PEOPLE

...AT LEAST FOR NOW...

HOOCHIE MAMA

SAY "NO!" TO NON-FAT DECAF LATTES

AND SAY "YES" TO BEING A BITCH.

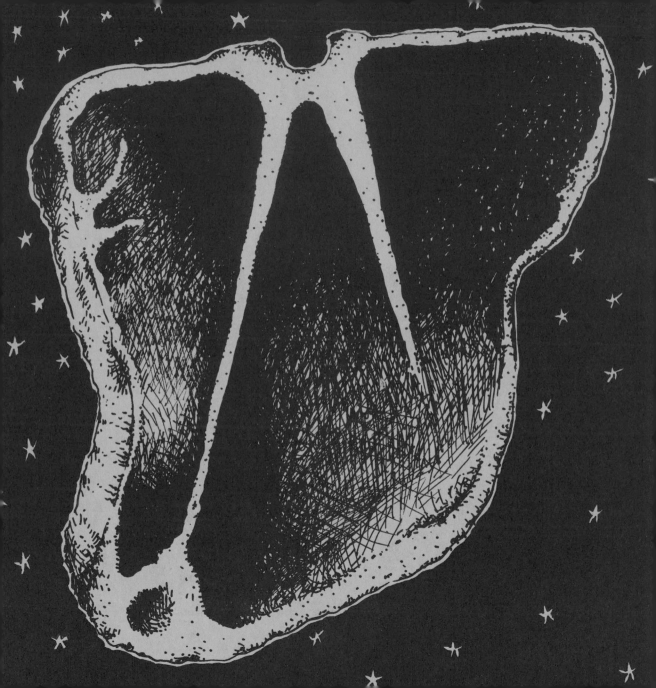

HOOCHIE · MAMA

We rented a house in West Virginia and when we moved in, we brought along our wooden notepad holder that was shaped like a small, old-fashioned children's sled. It was the kind of thing you hung next to the kitchen phone. You dropped a roll of paper in at the top, threaded it through a bar at the bottom and you were set to go. It was all about taking only what you needed when it came to Thanksgiving grocery lists or tiny local phone numbers. Nothing more/nothing less.

My mom, Debby, was thirty-two then, the same age I am now, and my sister, Elena Glane, was an unformed five. I was seven and learned how to crack eggs in that house. Mom taught us how to make sugar cookies. And so that we wouldn't be the subject of an urban myth, we used a wooden spoon instead of an electric mixer. When I was bad I got spanked with that same wooden spoon to keep me in line, so I sat on it to make it snap in half. After that, in a pinch, when I was bad she'd use her hot-pink hairbrush. But if my mom knew then how I'd turn into a demonic Monster Girl, she'd have not only made cookies with the electric mixer, but punished me with it as well.

Hindsight is always so 20/20.

Just down the hill from us was a brother and a sister who lived in a house that had a big hill as their whole backyard. It was covered by lush wild onions. Sometimes I'd pull off handfuls and inhale and wonder if we could make this stuff into soup in case of an emergency, like war.

The sister's name was Kim and I had a crush on her older brother because he had a blond bowl cut and wore wire-rimmed glasses. I can't remember his name right now, but he looked like a sensitive, chunky folksinger at a time in America's history when everyone in the country looked

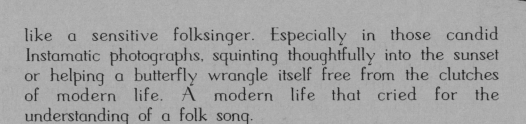

like a sensitive folksinger. Especially in those candid Instamatic photographs, squinting thoughtfully into the sunset or helping a butterfly wrangle itself free from the clutches of modern life. A modern life that cried for the understanding of a folk song.

Kim's brother had a lot of passion brewing under his Sears Toughskins from the Husky department, and I wanted to grow up and be the one to undo the zipper that would make me a Woman with a capital "w." I didn't need a poem, a song, or even nary a glance in my underaged direction. It was enough that he could make a different clubhouse every week out of the same musty, oniony wood and then share it with all of us without being such a dork. He liked the company. You see, he had the strong, silent image that the wildly successful cigarette industry was based on. "How insightful of them," I'd later admit.

When Halloween came around, some girl up the street made a haunted house in her basement, and yeah, she had the peeled grapes for eyes. To this day I still won't eat grapes.

We went trick-or-treating and got big Hershey bars and baggies of chocolate chip cookies. We dumped our loot on the hoods of cars and swapped candy like Kennedy

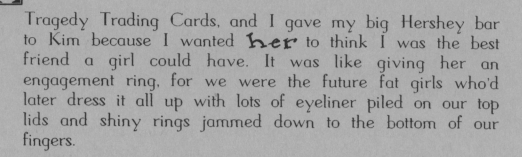

Tragedy Trading Cards, and I gave my big Hershey bar to Kim because I wanted **her** to think I was the best friend a girl could have. It was like giving her an engagement ring, for we were the future fat girls who'd later dress it all up with lots of eyeliner piled on our top lids and shiny rings jammed down to the bottom of our fingers.

We'd never become the kind of apologetic fat girls who knew our places in the bodily caste system—smiling too much, giving away cigarettes and letting people keep our Tupperware./I wonder if Kim still has her eyebrows, because back then you lost them along with your innocence. It was the price you paid for staying in West Virginia.

I was in second grade and the janitor at the school was an old hunched-over black man and his wife worked with him. Every day she wore an easy blue broadcloth muumuu, with rags, sponges, and gloves sticking out of the useful yellow patch pockets she'd stitched on after buying the muumuu.

They had this cramped, dark little office where they had a big old TV on the floor that played soft elevator music and had boring typewriter writing constantly going down a blue

or green screen, reporting the weather, community events, and school lunch menus.

Neither one of them talked much, but they smiled whenever they saw me and every once in a while the husband would lean his mop against the wall, wave me over to him, and hand me a small, sealed envelope to give to my mom.

He wrote little notes to her and I don't remember what they said, but he'd fold in a twenty-dollar bill for her to spend on my sister and me, just to help her out.

Mom made arts-and-crafty wall hangings in our house for the YWCA Christmas bazaar. She had a big round friend with no waist who made these crafts with her; this friend had lots of black eyeliner piled on her eyelids, and rings cinched at the bottom of her own short fingers like hose clamps.

We'd all go out to a Greek place called Lopez's Grill to eat pizza. We couldn't have soda in the house, but when we were at the grill, Elena and I got to drink as many RC Colas as we wanted because it kept us quiet while the adults talked. Since Elena wasn't even seven yet, she didn't have a whole lot of ideas as to what to talk about, so I'd quietly drink RC, listen to the jukebox, and wonder why

some guy would admit to shooting the sheriff but not the deputy. Why would he actually admit shooting anybody? I looked forward to the day when I'd finally understand. That day has yet to come.

My mom's round friend with eyeliner didn't like kids because she'd been an only child herself, and no matter how old she got, she didn't like having the attention off of her. But her parents once gave my sister and me a couple of Wrigley's Spearmint gum boxes that were taller than we were, so we didn't care how irritating she was when she harmonized to Streisand records like a Barbra shop quartet. I looked forward to the day when I'd finally understand America's pay-through-the-nose love for Barbra. That day has also yet to come.

Together, she and my mom made felt-snail wall hangings on yellow burlap with dowels at the top and a dab of cotton under the snail shells to make them more three-dimensional so they looked like they were popping right out at you. I was amazed and thought it was the most clever thing I'd ever seen.

Later in that summer, some of my friends ran over and banged on the aluminum screen door because my puppy, Mittens, had been hit by a car. I ran to her, but I felt so useless. She was panting, lying on her side with her tongue sticking out more than usual, and I didn't want to touch her and make anything worse inside of her. It was only a few minutes before she died. With such a fair mom who explained every spanking, it was the first time I just didn't get it/didn't understand why.

At bedtime that night I sat on Mom's double bed, crying as she tried like Sesame Street to explain the life and death things we never really understand until that very last minute when we're sprawled and gasping before the tires of our own deaths. She was trying to get ready for bed as she talked to me, but then she stopped fluffing her pillows and she started crying, too. Not like a grown-up mom tear or two, but her face got all wrinkled up and red and she was crying and crying, just like a kid. I was stunned. At first I wanted her to know everything and make it better, but then it turned out she wasn't so sure. It took me a minute to readjust my expectations from an omnipotent mother to a human mom. I loved her so much for not being that much older than me after all.

The next day in school, I sat in the bathroom stall and sobbed. As I unrolled the toilet paper to blow my nose, I promised myself I'd remember the date of Mittens's death forever, but now I'm not sure whether it was June 6 or even if it was a Monday.

Later that fall, when a spider moved into my bedroom window, I gave it a name, talked to it so it would feel welcome in my window. I wanted it to be safe there forever so it wouldn't get hit by a car.

A lot happened in the short time we lived in that house, and when the owner gave us notice to leave immediately so his grown-up kids could move in, my mom was mad and actually really scared by the realization that someone could suddenly make you move. So I got mad, too. I chose to fight back in the only way I knew how—by grabbing my crayons and quietly scribbling "you are bad pig people" all inside my bedroom closet. Since I had to get my crayons from Goodwill, I had a fraction of the crayons that I have today—and lo! what color combinations and meanings I could create with three crayons!

They ended up keeping part of Mom's security deposit because of it, and at first she turned around to me and laughed, but then she remembered how she wasn't my age after all and reprimanded me on how it was a bad, bad—*very bad*—thing to do.

But I'd already heard her laugh and seen the flash of pride in her eyes because I'd fought back. And forever addicted to the love of my mother, this is the story of how I grew up lap dancing for Mommy with a box of crayons in my hand, quietly writing the truth in the closet of bad pig people, the kind who always take so much more telephone notepad paper than they need, regardless of how small the local phone number is.

I looked forward to the day when I'd finally understand how the amazing trick is to do it so it doesn't come out of your own security deposit. That day did finally come. It was almost twenty-five years after my first crayon episode. When I was big enough to stop holding my crayons in my hands and could wedge them under my clamp-like breasts instead. It was during the summer when a tottering heir, John John Kennedy, and his tiny little wife fell down into the sea and she got so bloated after all those compliments. She looked down at her waterlogged blowfish ankles from heaven and was so horrified, she turned to stone.

La Otra Carne Blanca

"**H**ave a nice day," I called cheerfully to the bus driver on my way past her, on my way home from jail, but she didn't say anything. Maybe I was overly enthusiastic in poking her in the hip. Maybe it was because she was wearing brown and UPS drivers are the only ones who have a nice day wearing brown since everyone wants to have sex with them. UPS drivers knew that long gone were the days when people killed the messenger, because now everyone wanted to fuck the messenger.

I didn't know if anyone wanted to have sex with the bus driver, but her pockets were gaping out at the sides of her hips like *Hustler* beaver shots and I wanted to poke her there. What can I say? I am not made of stone. Open tissue boxes make me blush and I ravage my ears with Q-Tips until my eyes flutter and roll back in my head.

Who'd have ever thought anyone wearing the color of a cardboard box would be sexy? The one who came up with the idea had his fingers firmly crammed between America's giggling knees. FedEx may be dependable, more expensive—and therefore more elitist—but like other high-class things, they're just not sexy enough for a romp on the foyer rug. And while Airborne may be the least dependable, they are the most humorous and friendly. Alas, just like the friend you never want to sleep with.

Life may not be fair, but every once in a while it all really does come out in the wash. San Francisco used to have a population who had sex but they died off and the rest had just been evicted to give way to a generation of ambitious Latte People with secretary spread, who think they can take over the world with a computer platform shift. When they got undressed, what you saw most often wasn't cellulite. No, it was the textured weave of their office chairs.

Lattes are good. But Latte People are usually nouveau computer bohemians who think they're actually artists. This is more like spending a night in jail and calling yourself a P.O.W.

And the same way that cockroaches, Martha Stewart, and Oprah will be the only ones left to repopulate the world after the nuclear war, after the Silicon Valley boom, the UPS drivers were the only working class left in San Francisco who were having lots of actual sex with real people. And typically they were the "vockies" in high school who took the vocational classes and weren't sure what to do after graduation, and since they didn't inherit the luxury of sitting around, wasting their firm-breasted decades roaming

around the castle annoying the maids and crashing little airplanes into oceans for fun, they joined UPS instead.

But they're having the last monster-movie laugh. For a little carpal tunnel syndrome in exchange, these silent heroes of commerce in America spend all day acting like honeybees in big trucks, going from place to place, having sex in between delivering computer chips and boxes of money to companies so the rest of us can go online and have imaginary e-mail sex. And that's a good thing because the downside, of course, is that jerking off can be out of the question. Like trying to stroke yourself with an old dried-up monkey paw. It's almost as if the three ironic wishes had already been granted.

And the carpal tunnel the UPS drivers endured on the way to earning their own decadent routes of cheap sex meant that they had to clutch packages tightly between their wrists on the way to your door, but it also helped them cover the wet spots in their pants left there by that last lady who wore frilly ankle socks and a size 18 baby-doll dress./The one who tried to hide the small pile of stretch marks on her stomach, and called him "Daddy-o" in an old little girl's cancer-throated drawl.

This carpal tunnel from all that repetitive scanning means that they're also not real good at grabbing your tits—they can only fling their limp hands at your rock-hard nipples—but that's not what the housewives are answering the door for anyhow. And with three-minutes-per-address already figured out in their schedules, don't expect to come. Maybe later, through an erotic memory you can hold up like a flash card whenever you need to masturbate yourself senseless.

But no one was masturbating anymore—forget being a city that never slept, as New York is full of caffeinated people from Connecticut anyway—San Francisco had gone from being a city that used to toss its citizens' genitals in the air like batons to a city that only had time to read Dan Savage's canned-ham sex column about ingrown fetishes. Look at my mold.

So you see, after getting out of jail, I went back to my city, but my city wasn't there because it was suddenly too expensive for anyone interesting to live there. This is the story of what happened . . . why I'd ride back on my motorcycle in an invisible muumuu, fervently waving a box of crayons to save the city . . . It's the story of how the lone-riding UPS driver became king, and why receptionists everywhere were wiping delivery semen from the corners of their data-entry mouths with long fingernails as they curtly answered the phone: "Blah blah dot-com Incorporated."

And it's also the story of bored and disillusioned suburbanites who find poverty as fascinating as an old freak show with a two-headed baby floating in a jar of formaldehyde. And while the shrinking middle class is busy checking the sofa cushions for change, they're getting clubbed like baby seals for the trendy jackets with the embroidered name tags.

It's the story of screaming renters getting dry-fucked, falling to their knees crying "uncle!" and how their screams got lost in the mail.

That's the way history is. We all get lost in the phone books of time and we all lose our girlish figures. We all get the chance to become the scary one the children would run from and tell campfire stories about. We *all* get our turn. Oh, yes, we do—and don't you forget it. Even if you manage to go out in a decapitated head-on-collision blaze of glory in your baby-skinned thirties. Because not only does no one get out of here alive, no one gets out of here *pretty*. We all go the way of the Vikings, and so, too, passed the people in San Francisco who used to actually have sex.

Without having sex, I jumped down off the last step on the bus. It left me at Market Street where the Masturbation Parade used to take place, replaced by a daily Ford Explorer/Yukon Denali parade. I could've waited for another bus to take me closer to my place, but walking the few miles with a prison-issue duffel slung over my shoulder seemed like a cowboy-song way of coming home to San Francisco, the flamboyant City of Second Chances.

I'd just gotten released from Zucchini Cave, the pet name for a women's detention center where the aluminum was painted appliance green to match our clothes and we passed infections around like mashed potatoes. I would later type, xerox, then hand staple my prison memoir, *They Call Me Mad Dog*, and give it away on street corners while the fingerprint ink was still wet on my fingers. They thought I'd murdered my ex-girlfriend, but I'd only kidnapped her for a second, I swear, but that's another story altogether.

As I loped deeper into the heart of the Mission, everything seemed the same at first. There were still colorful murals covering the sides of buildings and Victorian houses in jelly-bean colors like turquoise, purple, magenta, or painted with leftover glossy swimming-pool-blue paint, with impromptu crooked windows all along the outsides, and still just a few broken-down cars along the street.

But evil lurked, crossed its legs, laughed that creepy little monster-movie cackle and waited for me to make it home. . . .

The funky Victorians gave way to make-believe "live/work" artist lofts. Lofts used to be a converted industrial space with a bathroom in it. Now they're just studio apartments with high ceilings. Ticky-tacky houses/the tract homes of today. Instead of the aqua green corrugated plastic that surrounded suburban swimming pools, they've just painted it silver so it looks like corrugated steel.

The crayon-colored Victorians also slowly gave way to homeowner association palettes of paint labeled Manifest Destiny Gray, trimmed in Conquistador Slate Gray, Trail of Tears Teal, or *shhhh, quiet* shades of pantyhose beige to cover the intricate varicose veins of intricate wiring of intricate, complicated lives of intricate people who didn't need people, but needed those intricate little Maxipad phones on which they could talk to people who could help get them more things to impress the people they never needed in the first place.

All this was spreading across the landscape like a deadly San Francisco aluminum fog, decimating actual artists' lofts—even covering houses they'd neglected to tear down first. And Mexican families, metal-head lesbians, artists, and old folks were being evicted and so they ran, ran, ran as fast as they could away from the Silicon Valley Latte People, frantically tearing across the bridges for their lives like the chick in the woods in those slasher horror movies. Tits bounced, mascara ran.

Gentrification was now about being safe. Pounding out anything that was gonna cause a ripple.

I saw the mayor, Willy Beige, the only black person in downtown San Francisco, who looked like a dapper little pimp-daddy in a fedora and Italian-made suit, jump out of his limousine to erect chain stores in the last black neighborhood so that mothers could have $6.50/hour cashier positions forever, and when he was done, he wrestled the shopping carts from the homeless so the new citizens would think they were the happy-go-lucky sort who carried their belongings in bandannas at the end of sticks and sang "Zippity doo da" along the train tracks.

"For Rent" signs told me how the last of the city's tenacious renters were evicted for the slightest infractions, like pets farting too much, so the apartment could be rented out for four, five, and seven times more to people wearing sitcom hairstyles and sporting the vaudevillian sense of justice that comes with it.

They also spoke of how broken-down houses were routinely selling for over a half-billion and Realtors were so excited they nearly peed themselves while flipping through the white pages, cold-calling folks to ask if they wanted to sell their houses, too. No matter how ridiculously high the original asking price, it *always* got higher bids. The practice was becoming customary.

"One hell of an informative rental sign," you say, and you're right. Those were the days. The days when rental signs could give you the lowdown, while bottle caps and tea bags told us how to live, with Thoreau giving way to Darwinistic affirmations that said, *"Come on, old man! Get up off the ground or I'll fuck you right there."*

The "For Sale" signs spoke to me of how these new faux-loft condos *started* at $500,000,000 for each miniature, single person's unit, and ranged up to a trillion and more for two bedrooms, for those who wanted home offices. What made them so profitable was that they were built on cheap industrial land while being the most expensive housing in the city.

The "live/work loft" commercial-zoning label exempted developers and buyers from affordable housing requirements, school taxes, and a bouquet of fees. They were so excited by this hula-hoop loophole, they had to control themselves from twirling around, humming happy songs with drippy Popsicles in their mouths, because from beginning to end, it was a great big Wesson-oiled "yesssss": Not only was the land cheap to begin with, but to the retail loft buyers, the more industrial and austere the units looked, with concrete floors, exposed beams, and aluminum windows, the more they clamored for a clean and safe authentic urban carnival ride where the minimum height requirement was financially quite high.

Sushi bars had spread around the edges of the neighborhood like bread mold. Used diapers no longer blew around the streets like sagebrush. I passed them by, just me, my duffel, and a brand-new, working-class future staggering for footing. I was young, but I knew enough to know that where there is sushi and the little neatly rolled up and arranged attitudes to go with it, there are usually cappuccino frappes to wash it all down afterward. The Gap and Starbucks are the ghetto liquor stores of the yuppie neighborhoods.

The few remaining people in ill-fitting used clothing danced and hopped around the city's fault lines, doing the magical earthquake dance with lottery tickets in their teeth—if a big, scary earthquake didn't clear the city, then maybe they'd win enough millions to at least put a down payment on one of those live/work things.

hen I finally got home, there were a couple of those new Saltine-box lofts on either side of my shack. Their expensive shadows blocked out the sun and my working-class future, but in the darkness, I spotted a couple of salivating developers ogling, catcalling, and smooching at my single-unit shack with raging real estate hard-ons, wringing their hands greedily as if they were rubbing in the lotion of success.

My old motorcycle was there, waiting for me in front of my place, covered in spiderwebs, covered in black city grit, with pieces of paper taped and tucked all over her, fluttering in the wind, waving me home to the finish line. But these papers didn't say "welcome home," or "we love you," or "for a good time come to Aggie's birthday party." No. Because is there anyone around here named Aggie anymore? No, those children had been evicted from my block, replaced by babies who'd been lulled to sleep with John Philip Sousa so they'd march out of the womb with blind ambition and no free time. Babies named Taylor and Ashley who're lactose intolerant and allergic to wheat and kitty cats and get ear infections. Pale, splotchy children squinting at the sun who looked like they'd never make it, but would live to grow up, annoy the maids and crash airplanes.

The faded papers flapping in the wind **Were** an archive of months of frustration and the new wave of puckered intolerance and suburban brutality: the same ironic people who used to write covenant newsletters about abolishing front yard flamingoes, while lamenting the lack of community, moved to the cities for fun, and demanded that the nightclubs hush up and keep it down, and now they wanted me to move my bike. They used the kind of clenched-jaw "please"s that sounded more like very well-practiced legal threats.

It was becoming apparent that San Francisco was turning into a corporate campus. The kind where you went to the company store for a blanket and got docked on your Visa card and had the money deducted from your wages. And if you were a dot-com person working in Silicon Valley, you were working long days and sleeping under your desk, using that same blanket to keep you warm and convince you that sacrificing your youth for three-hour commutes, a corporate personal life, lots of money and stock options was all worth it.

I was the last of the *Mujer* Ricans, just about surrounded by computer programmers on all four sides, and a lot of them never even left their houses. These were the folks who

were filling the void left by all the gay artists who died in the eighties and nineties. When the computer programmers left their houses, instead of having sex with UPS drivers like the last guys, their eyes quickly darted away from neighbors like their ingrown sex drives and they scampered through these gentrified streets of fear like screen savers.

Books, newspapers, and magazines gushed about Silicon Valley's stars, much like *Teen Beat* magazine rhapsodizes over the latest chick/dick for a day. Everything comes so fast and easy here, from orgasms to true love to financial success, and everyone feels like a goddamned genius even though they're nothing more than a bunch of Fred Flintstones smacking their bellies and giving advice to everyone about how to make it big, real big.

Technical folks around here are not internationally famous for their social skills. They pick their noses on dates and snort when they tell scatological jokes, and I won't even mention what the boys are like.

But I guess if I was paying $75,000 a month for a two-bedroom apartment, I'd never leave it either, because I'd want to get my money's worth. I'd spend all weekend ejaculating all over the hardwood floors and sliding through all the rooms on garbage bags.

A garbage bag blew across my feet. And THAT, along with the BATTLE CRY of sushi,* should've told us all that WE needed to know.

BUT AS YOU KNOW,
iT DOESN'T EVER START
OR END WITH SUSHI.
SUSHI
is merely a FISHY
BATTLE CRY
...FOR A NEW
ERA

My friend Bark Flammers kept my cat for me while I was in jail and afterward would only let me have visitation rights. It was just as well, because after I got out of jail, I was so broke, every time I pet her I thought of hors d'oeuvres. I felt Donner Pass shame.

Anyway, Bark had made a killing after showing up on Oprah with his *Eat Me* revenge book full of tips. When it got optioned for a big Hollywood tearjerker that Robin Williams would direct, produce, and play every single part—including the pets—he bought a couple of rental properties over on the next block, and instantly rented them at market rate without even double-checking the door keys.

To celebrate, Bark went to Farallon, a restaurant famous for its amazing service, where a 20 percent tip quickly rounds out to $500. And because he was trying to lose weight, he just sat at the table with his untouched salad and a sweaty glass of Tab with melting ice cubes floating on the top, and asked the waiters to brush his hair.

Like so many thin and beautiful women, he went home pretty but hungry. So he drank expensive cognac, ate fat-free cookies and filet mignon for days until he was so backed up, he paid dearly for Darjeeling tea high colonics alternated with back massages and shopping sprees. In his own little Valley of the Dolls, he popped Propecia and Viagra like breath mints and started smoking expensive cigars that made him cough up pink stars, yellow moons, and green clovers. He said his life was so damn good, he smoked cigars because he needed something, anything, to complain about. So he complained about them choking more minutes out of his life expectancy.

When I first met him, he was a simple man with a thriving phone-in revenge business. A man who'd been raised by a pack of stoic Catholics in Michigan. A man brought up on squirrel and moose, in a place where they swerved *toward* roadkill. Like most of us, his dreams were simple. He dreamed of having sex with black men, handing out towels at a boxing club, and saying things like "Be sure to clean those special secret places, boys, cause Mama's gonna check." And when he got old, Bark wanted to open a Club Med for dogs and have a saffron and caper farm.

Then later, as his stocks rose, his sex drive shrank but he tried to smack it to attention like the rest of the workaholics in town.

Bark's forty-three and goes to a Gold's Gym that looks like a Blanche DuBois showboat casino with treadmills to prevent aging and soft pink 40-watt bulbs to hide what's already happened. Like most baby boomers, he's actually succeeding. This is a generation with no Great Depressions to exacerbate turkey neck, or World Wars to pull at the delicate eye skin. Their traumas are mostly internal, or self-inflicted, and can quickly be fixed with the first few pages of best-selling self-help books.

Boomers are like the Jews of Time, believing that theirs is the only chosen generation, and that they actually will take it *all* with them. Fortunately, every once in a while we're lucky enough to have some girl sleep in a thousand-year-old redwood so they can't make a deck out of it.

Strange stuff is always happening to Bark because he walks his pit bull in the park three times a day and bends over to scoop her evil pellets into a plastic bag. Since she's cute, packed tight into her skin and struts high on the balls of her paws, and has a growl that sounds like a child's wrist caught in a garbage disposal, he calls her his little Puerto Rican girl. Writing on her man's car in lipstick is nothing. With this dog, it was not merely a question of whether her glass was half full or empty, but whether it'd been smashed against the curb so the shards could be used to carve your heart out and bury it under the floorboards.

He figures this is what it must've been like for my mother to raise me and he whispers a "Hail Mary" to my mom.

He meant to name her "Cha Cha," but somewhere got it wrong and now calls her "Chocha," which means "vagina" in Spanish. Maybe that's because I started calling her that, I don't know.

Anyway, Bark often gets in fights with other dog owners because he doesn't train Chocha and sometimes she tries to rip out the throat of someone's runway model Afghan dog, or disembowel a middle-aged mother's toddler, but like any mother of Pure Evil, he yawns and insists the dog was only playing, and that she's actually cute and sweet and gentle. Like when they're cuddling and watching death-row prison dramas on TV.

"There I was, minding my own business, when one of those man-hating lesbian incubators came up to me holding her sperm-bank child, crying and yelling at me to put a muzzle on my little dog. My sweet little Chocha. I said, 'Don't blame your kid's ugly face on *my* little dog; you should've seen the sperm donor photo first.'

"So then she has the gall to ask what my dog's still chewing on then, and I told the lady, 'Hey, none of your goddamn business but it's not the missing piece of your kid's turkey baster face! Look around you, Walmart shopper—this is a damn *city*. Consider yourself lucky this time: there are all sorts of broken glass, child molestors, and danger lurking out there, licking their chops, waiting for your pretty little boneless child.' "

So he told her she'd better take her ugly kid to the vet and leave him alone before he beat them to a bloody pulp.

"Heck, *I* was the one who was the victim here. It got me so stressed-out I felt sick and had to go to the sauna and get a massage before dinner."

When he wasn't having overprotective parents threaten him with lawsuits or vandalism, he was trading erotic massages with anyone who wasn't in on the economic boom. I think he liked that he didn't have to feel financially competitive around them and constantly talk about what else he was buying like with other businessmen who compared new watches. Bark loved buying stuff, but wasn't real good at keeping track of what he bought, so he often bought the same thing over and over again. Yuppies call this collecting.

One of his friends, Timber, he met during a **dog-fight.**

"See," he explained after introducing himself and shaking Bark's hand after the bad ꙰Dog fight, "if two pit bulls are going at it, you've got to grab one's tail and jam your thumb up the ass like so." Timber demonstrated. "It's distracting."

"You just did that now?" Bark sniffed the hand that'd shaken Timber's and flinched.

Timber once pulled out his penis for Bark and later pulled out his teeth for the Democrats. The penis part was in Bark's SUV; afterward, Bark dropped him off at the car he was living in, on the east side of Potrero, over by the famous guy who builds robots and blows them up. The guy's missing a thumb, but it's been replaced by his toe that's a different, colder temperature and still grows toe hair. You get used to the blasts as if they were police sirens. White noise.

As for how Timber lost his teeth, one of the old liberals in social services said something like, "Hey, your teeth are really rotting there, aren't they?" And they were. They were dark brown like tiny old tea bags, and so someone patted him on the head and said, "We want to give you all new teeth; a brand-new start."

Each one of those tea-bag teeth got plucked out of his homeless little head, like she loves me/she loves me not, and because of some bureaucratic mistake where they went over the budget, they suddenly didn't remember saying anything about putting them back. Now his mouth caves in. This is a fascinating story of how yet another one of us stopped being pretty.

Timber's young, thirtyish, but not feeling quite so fresh anymore. He's got thinning light brown hair combed back to reveal a high forehead and thick glasses. His eyes have an intelligent, observant, lecherous feel. I think with so many genius people those qualities go hand in hand. And he constantly wants to have sex with Bark, so when exposing himself wasn't enough to make Bark's face fall into his lap, he gave Bark a short pile of stuck-together photographs of himself naked with cock rings and a leg of beige pantyhose pulled over his head, squishing his features like a bank robber. It was very scary, because every time you leafed through them, another layer of the photograph ripped away. Just like Bark's real estate appraisals after they dried and he proudly handed them to me to see how much more the house was worth.

I begged Bark to give back the pictures, because they were in a little plastic shelf under the car radio, and I don't usually give a damn about what people think, but it made me worry about someone later finding our fingerprints on them.

Bark was so excited about the real estate market, he stopped having his Lycra-covered genitals appraised and tugged on by strangers in saunas, and turned to having his properties appraised and tugged on by professionals every other week. You see, in the same way that the UPS guys were king with the sex-starved receptionists, a real estate appraiser could caustically insult a homeowner about a badly constructed room addition and leave with a blow job and an extra one in his pocket for later.

Oh, and there was *plenty* of bad construction. Plenty. Bark said Levi's, tool belts, and knee pads were gay lingerie, and then he picked his contractors based on their skin softness, and so construction on his house ended up looking more like the set from a gay porn movie.

Calling up his stockbroker with a hand wedged down the front of his tastefully simple winter-white butt thong was all the love he needed. And sex for Bark became scheduling estimates with the real estate appraiser guy who made judgments in a fake German accent and wrote things down.

The first time the fake German real estate appraiser swaggered up to his door, Bark demurely emerged, pulling the door back with his naked, tan, and shiny knee. Samba music gushed forth, lightly brushing the appraiser's thigh on its way down the stairs like latte foam. He offered a lit cigar and warm brandy with one hand, and offered his other hand in introduction.

"CALL ME HONDO," Bark Flammers exhaled a little too loudly. So loudly the neighbors would, from that point on, refer to him as "HONDO," and later tell me this very story in its entirety.

Hours of lap dancing later, HONDO opened the door and waved good-bye with his written appraisals chronologically wedged into the waistband of his winter-white butt thong, like relatively crisp five-dollar bills.

It wasn't until the taillights could no longer be seen that he'd close every curtain and let the phone ring for the next two hours while dancing up against his real estate appraisals.

HONDO Flammers was getting in on the melting Popsicle dance where when you have to pee you don't want to go to the bathroom because everything's so great and you can't stand to miss a single thing. You could ask so much for rent, he decided to just rent his own house out for $250,000 a month and go to the Marriott, have little Thai boys lick his feet and insist how natural his hair implants looked.

I developed a love-hate relationship with the few homeless left who slept in front of the house; they kept me up much of the night, but by simply being there, I imagined that they were holding down the last little, threadbare corner on a real estate market akin to Cabbage Patch Beanie Baby fervor: "Two thousand for the stupid duck."

I woke up free, looking outside my little window. Originally I'd wanted to bite the day in the ass, but ended up gumming the morning instead because it was unusually rainy outside. The Mission's typically the sunniest place in the city when everywhere else is foggy, but not this day. I lived right near the highway and the on- and off-ramps, and with all the cars speeding by it sounded like a distant cheering crowd.

I'd left the window open on top, oh maybe ten inches, back before I'd gone to jail. No one had closed it. In the meantime, a spider had built a pretty web on top and even though it was rainy and pretty damn windy, I just didn't have the heart to shut the window and ruin the web.

My sister, Elena Glane, hated wasps, and I was there the last time she went nuts and threw boxes of frozen vegetables at one, finally killing it an hour later. After

pulling the rubble off of its little mashed and twisted black-and-yellow body, she suddenly looked back at me with stark shame that reached to the back of this country's past. She bent over, clutched her stomach, and fell to her knees beside the crumpled wasp, quietly admitting, "I feel like a cop who killed a black kid."

I'd be fine with the window open. So I pulled out the down sleeping bag I once got by forging a bad roommate's check in Philadelphia. She moved out when I wasn't home and took a lot of my things but forgot to forward her mail. Let's just say that somehow I got myself a *very nice* sleeping bag.

The wind eventually tore the spider's web apart and I fell back to sleep all cuddled up. I felt bad for the spider and wished I could give her some kind of emergency housing, but they like those webs. That's cuddling for them—all suspended, with the wind blowing past.

The radio alarm clock was still set to go off every morning, so I woke up to National Public Radio reporting on African guys who were spooging inside of infant virgin girls in Africa with mutilated genitals so their AIDS would go away and come again some other day.

I mentally covered my ears and thought "La! La! La!", clicked the radio off, and turned back to the window to see the spider dropping down from the top of the window with her string ⟿ she was totally rebuilding her web.

I don't know why she insists on keeping it there, because I've never seen other spiders catch anything in that space. She was like my own window screen to keep the other bugs out. And then I was thinking that I'd help her out and catch a fly—I hate flies—and hold it up to the web. But the thought of not even giving a fly a chance made me feel evil, like if I came back as a fly, I was really gonna pay for that one. Plus, flies are hard to catch. And I didn't want to insult the spider and insinuate that she didn't know what she was doing by staying there in the first place.

Maybe it's a guy spider. I actually think it's a guy spider. There are no eggs sitting there near the ripped-up web. Do guy spiders make webs? Maybe this one is inspired by constant rebuilding. Maybe it's a chunky blond spider with a bowl cut and wire-rimmed glasses. Do spiders live like single people? You never hear of spider clans or packs of spiders. I suppose they're solitary, pensive creatures. They're so gentle when they're not typecast in movies as brutal murderers.

I also leave them in my shower until I need a bottle of whatever it is they've built webs on. I scoop them up with matchbook covers and put them outside. But then some people came and tore off all the ivy on the outside of the building, so there I am again, sending little creatures to their deaths.

That's the story of me trying to be a decent landlord.

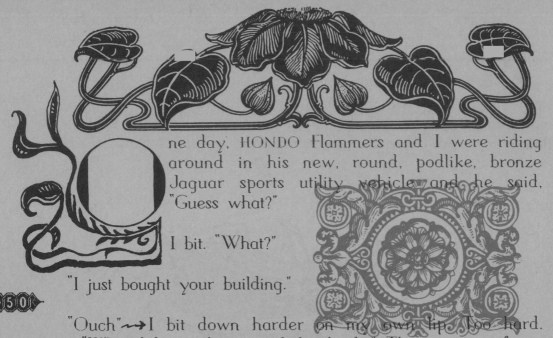

ne day, HONDO Flammers and I were riding around in his new, round, podlike, bronze Jaguar sports utility vehicle, and he said, "Guess what?"

I bit. "What?"

"I just bought your building."

"Ouch"⟿I bit down harder on my own lip. Too hard. ⟿"Why did you buy *my* little shack?" The contents of my stomach curdled at the taste of my own blood.

HONDO waved my concern away like a fly. "Just an investment, don't worry about it. I won't be asking you to leave, or anything . . . At least not right now," he said lightly, while scanning the road. "It's all about building up my portfolio for my retirement next year. Now"—from under his seat he handed me a new Brooks Brothers catalogue, featuring a sweaty rugby player look, and pointed to some Ivy League model who resembled Oscar Wilde's lover—"what do you think of these pants in this university color? I already have them in polo field green, foxhunt red, and blueblood morning mist."

" 'University' is not a color, HONDO."

"Sure it is. Makes all the sense in the world." He poked at a photo of a stack of the folded pants in assorted colors. "This one." He circled with his finger. "Like the brick of a university building." Or a scab.

"Then wouldn't that be more like 'foxhunt red'?"

"No, foxhunt red is the color *after* the foxhunt."

"Ew, of course." I cringed. Inside, I was crying like a sad little clown, but outside, I was smiling, smiling, and smiling some more, telling him with my heart that it was a lovely color. And that was that. Who was he?

Then I told him that I had to build my own life back up, so I asked him for a $10,000 loan so I could start my fake-penis empirette back up again.

"Let's start that sentence all over again. Like, what's in it for me? C'mon, Rodriguez, repeat after me—"

"—Look, HONDO, if I do real well..." I explained that he wouldn't even have to get around to asking me to leave.

He nodded at the road and then said, "Yes, sounds like a good investment, since there's been a lull in dick art lately." He handed me the pile of Timber's photos. "Welcome back. Hey, and consider this a house-worming gift." He laughed.

I whimpered.

"What?" He demanded. *"Why are you staring* at me like that? You look like you've just seen a ghost. Stop it or I'll beat you to a bloody pulp, Rodriguez. You're creeping me out."

No, Mr. HONDO. You're creeping me out with that non-fat, decaf latte attitude of yours. The signs were all lined up. His sex drive had gone down the road with his penis against his shoulder like a fishing pole, whistling the *Andy Griffith* theme song, and the message was clear. More and more, he was becoming one of

THEM

FEAR of A YAHOO PLANET

I had the blues, so I went to the San Francisco Blues Festival with my carpet-licking friends named after things: Chair, Jean, and Rose. I hadn't seen them since I'd gone to jail. Like all rugs, they'd had a little slap n' tickle with each other at some time or another, and they'd all recently been evicted. So Rose won the lottery and only had enough to cover that month's electric bill and buy a one-bedroom condominium just outside of San Francisco, in Daly City, the place that inspired the old "Ticky-Tacky Houses" song.

They all lived there together with her gorgeously confused six-foot-eleven-inch son who wasn't sure what he wanted to do with his life yet even though he wasn't inheriting airplanes to crash into the sea. We all wondered: would he become a UPS driver?

Chair was about fifty, and born with her foot in her mouth. Speaking of her feet, once I asked her if she liked thong sandals and she answered, "Why would I want anything between my toes if I don't even like floss between my teeth or men between my legs? Don't you have two pieces of flesh I can stick something in between?" She grabbed my foot and pushed her finger back and forth between my big toe and the next one. "There. Does that feel good? Do you have butt thongs, too?"

Like me, she spent a lot of her free time apologizing or explaining what she'd said to someone. She was from San Francisco and that's all she'll let me repeat. Her life's a great big secret. In fact, she doesn't want anyone to know that she's even here, so let's move on to Jean.

Jean has a great big blond ponytail and is so cool she has never had a motorcycle without a kickstart. Jean doesn't talk much because she's not much for apologizing all about it later. She's usually the one who taps Chair or me on the shoulder for one of us to go over and apologize about something.

Rose is a fashionable nurse who vomits at the sight of vomit, and wears blood-colored cat eyeglasses and scrubs with miniature skulls printed on them. So tiny, they're mostly subliminal. She figures it reminds her patients they're lucky to be alive and keeps needless whining down. She's the mother to us all, and is the one we're usually apologizing to. She drove in a car and the rest of us took our motorcycles.

Somehow, Chair smokes while she's riding a motorcycle and she says, "Nothing like a cigarette in your mouth and a bike between your legs." Last I heard, she was trying to quit.

On our way to the blues festival, she made a mistake up one of those tall San Francisco hills, and flipped backward off her bike. She landed on her stomach and barely got a bruise. She's my Jack LaLanne inspiration and that's how I wanna do fifty. She warned me, "But when you turn fifty-five, you get a senior citizen discount and a free bag of skin tags."

She barely ever gets tired and she's beautiful and funny. She's got cheekbones so sharp you could slice hard cheese with them. When she gets sick, she's well in ten minutes. When she twists her ankle, she powers over it and walks up hills and picks up her dog's feces without complaining. That's when I call her "stump walker"; she makes those half her age look thick-ankled and lazy. Chair attributes it all to her Polish peasant genes.

HONDO Hammers really thinks she might be one of those Über People the Nazis were trying to breed. He says, "Fiftyish? She's Polish? Hmm . . . think about it. They were over there trying to create the master race with *Polish* whores. Really, and she's *just the right age* . . ."

It's like she's my big sister and she says I'm her little pipsqueak. She verbally tickles me until I almost pee myself or spit out my soda. If I'm in her car, she stops just in time and says, "Hey—don't spew on my windows and don't wet the seat. I can't have the younger generation wetting my seat."

She's the one who taught me a few things to fine-tune what few manners I actually have: one's elder gets the crusty heel of the bread, while the young take the seats facing the wall at the dinner table. She also says that until a person grows up and gets a brain, they're like puppies. "Nothing cuter than a puppy and that's a good thing because they're always shitting everywhere and ripping the crotches out of panties." Chair says the only thing that makes young people bearable is that they're pretty; even the ugly ones.

I understood, because I found it hard to make it through the tirades of a twenty-year-old without bitterly glaring at my watch as they wasted what little time I had left on earth.

So there we were at this festival of pain, where happy couples are everywhere, ignoring the songs of love gone

bad. Chair said you could get secondhand smoke just from listening to music like this.

It's funny how when you're not used to seeing something, you go "ew." Maybe I was in the women's jail too long, but when I see heterosexuals holding hands I wince. Now, I don't feel like tying them to VW convertibles with rainbow stickers on the back window and dragging them until they're dead, but it just seems strange in a way, even though I'd been having those heterosexual fantasies. Yeah, you got it. Heterosexual fantasies. Go figure. It seemed so dirty. I won't tell any of my lesbian friends because they'd never share a soda with me again, as they'd say they wouldn't be able to trust where my mouth has been, and Chair will threaten to come over and wake me up by poking a broom handle in my back like a morning man.

So there we are at the festival. We've got a nice, healthy cushion of breathing space around us with invisible masking tape, and we're all cozy, when all of a sudden, about seven of these straight and narrow "Just Pettin' It, George" people plopped right down in front of us with these big ol' light purple beach chairs with a Yahoo! corporate logo on them. I guess you could've even called them lavender. . . .

Lavender is sweet. Makes you think of translucent old grandladies, sachets in underwear drawers, once-affordable apartments. Yahoo! and lavender together appeared as unthreatening as a pit bull licking a baby kitty clean.

So we're sitting there with these Latte People in Yahoo chairs in front of us, blocking our view, and I wouldn't have minded them so much, but the thing I don't like about them is that you can't see through them. They're transparent yet they block the view. They're short little shits, but they cast a long shadow in the rental market. A little clump of them—what's a clump of yuppies? A gaggle? Anyway, they're being wacky in that twenty-nothing suburban way, laughing, flirting, and kicking back bottled water and Starbuck's coffees, frappuccinos, and crapuccinos with those plastic domed Space Needle tops.

But when their cell phones started ringing, it all suddenly seemed too much like a metaphor for what was happening in the Mission, and I wondered why these yupwazee people not only had to cause other people the blues, but appropriate the blues in an academic postmodern way in which they could never feel blue while their cell phones are ringing, stocks are soaring, their lawn chairs are creaking, and they're blocking the view with their baseball caps

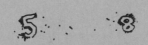

backward with the little dot-com logos. And with all of this gritty harmonica rage, all hell broke loose . . .

. . . I reached over and tapped the little girl on the shoulder. Pure bone covered in 100 percent chain-store cotton.

I knew that shoulder. I knew it well, from consoling a cigarette-smoking bulimic in the girls' bathroom in high school. Girls like these in high school were always draped against Jersey Camaros because they were too light-headed and faint from sugar lows to stand without leaning against a wall, a man, a something. They had to smoke a cigarette just to get enough of a nicotine rush to make it across the parking lot, and the reason they were always giving their boyfriends hickeys and blow jobs is because they were trying to leech salt and protein from their skin. Then they'd suck on locks of their hair like carnivores sucking out bone marrow.

How do I know? I consoled girls like these until they started looking at me as if I were a roast chicken. These girls loved their nutrient-rich men hard with a hunger that burned white-hot like a yeast infection in August.

Chair said, "1967? Nothing happened AFTER you were born → Except macramé. Even pillbox hats were over."

I asked the Yahoo people to either move over or leave and go back to Silicon Valley and take their calls there. I thought it'd be a cinch because I had that quietly psychotic look of Chihuahua hatred. "And *this* is probably why you read emergency room stories about cell phones trapped in people's rectums," I hissed at her. She looked puzzled, as if she hadn't heard the same urban legends.

But the girl proved to be a little hundred-pound pistol with a firmly entrenched suburban sense of entitlement and she yelled at me—entirely through her nose—explaining how it was an important call, "and hey—don't get your pink triangle all up in a wad," she finished. Then she agreed to turn off her phone.

My friend Jean patted me on the shoulder and raised her eyebrows. "Uh-oh, it looks like *someone* needs a nap."

"I don't need a nap," I hissed.

And Chair told me, "For someone who has no control of her upper and lower lips, let me just say that I hope you have tight underwear on so you can get control of at least one set of lips." She rubbed me lovingly and soothingly on the back. "Hey, why don't you go grow up, and pick up

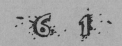

some change with your pussy? Or teach us how to make a shank with toenail clippings?"

"No way," I stuck out my jaw and said. "You need me to save you from the dark evil that surrounds us."

"I'm fifty-two, pipsqueak. When I need your help about puberty, then I'll ask for your help." She and Jean laughed and laughed as if doom wasn't staring them right in the face with a little doctor's flashlight, telling them to say "aaah," but living in San Francisco is all about San Andreas denial anyway, so I knew they needed me to stick around and flick away the oppression.

"Where's your nipple so I can tweak it?" I reached around, pulling on her sweatshirt. She had the nicest tits, but she usually hid them behind large starched shirts. Maybe it was because she couldn't store any pencils under them; who's to know?

She squirmed away in the cool way only Chair could and with her chin clenched to her chest, she managed, "Hey, go get your own pipsqueaks and take it out on them. Didn't you have your own little pipsqueak in jail?"

I turned away from Chair's little perky breasts and our little Yahoo girl was more demonic than we ever could've imagined. She and her tucked-in Banana Republic boyfriend started cuddling on the ground in front of us like a couple of corporations, and when the back of her shirt rode up around her armpits, I could see the spine bones above her ass like a string of ball bearings under her skin, bigger than her breasts. These two rolled around like logs in the water, picking affectionately at each other like baboons picking off lice.

Oh, but that was Fritos compared to when she stuck her little computer-programming finger in his ear canal and started poking around in a touching-earwax-equals-love equation.

She might've been one of the groupies following UPS drivers on their routes as if they were the Grateful Dead, following with a box of Q-Tips, cleaning the ears of UPS drivers for free so they can hear car horns.

I was afraid she'd show how devoted she was by sticking her finger in her mouth, and when she endearingly squeezed the Yahoo blackheads on his nose and showed him the loot as if she were a cat bringing him a trophy of cute trapped oil deposits, I thought I was gonna implode.

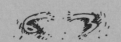

Oh what a fearful sight: where Puerto Rican bisexuality and Silicon Valley heterosexuality meet. Very scary. Almost as scary as a lesbian businesswoman.

I suddenly realized that this is how little heterosexual girls showed their love. I know we're all different: gay men show their love by telling you who else they're having sex with, while lesbians show their love by actually not telling you who they're even *thinking* of having sex with. Women and our need to talk about everything. We really must learn to confide in plants.

Ask yourself how do you really show your love. The answer may make you not so readily cast stones at me when I admit that I'd show my love by rimming that special someone, but I'd call it "squeezin' my tongue," because you've gotta admit, it just sounds better. Anuses feel like Life Savers circling your tongue, except for the minty-fresh part. Gettin' your tongue squeezed can say so much more than writing sonnets or giving back massages. That's too easy. Too passé now. And here I am, moving at the speed of light on the edge of the fashion of Love.

Anyway, Jean told me to look away and she dragged me away and bought me another drink, something pricey on the rocks, and I didn't even have to rim her. That is

friendship. Chair saw how emotionally touched I was and reached for my hand. "You're not gonna start crying, are you? Let's hope we can get through today without you crying, okay, kiddo?" She kissed me on the forehead and smiled. "You're so leaky. You leak all over the place. It's no wonder you're one of those female-ejaculators. A virgo's nightmare."

I'd seen that same sad, wavering smile on my mother a million times. The frightened smile, and the exhaustion of having a little daughter who might snap at any moment like a pit bull. It was the wavering smile of love and worry that came out whenever she left me at the baby-sitter's and she quietly pleaded with me by the screen door, "And please, kiddo, please don't crayon the closet. Okay, Mommy's gotta go. Honey, please don't grab my pantyhose like that, please . . . ouch, let go, sweetheart . . ." My poor mom. I was like a lumbering, evil, retarded kid who never knew when to stop petting mice to death or pulling on her nice work clothes.

"No." Through clenched teeth, I reassured Chair. "I'm going to enjoy my drink, listen to the music, and we'll relax on this grassy knoll."

All those alive on November 1963 looked at each other in silence.

"Uh-oh, now you've gone and done it," Jean said.

"What? I'm sorry, Rose," I quickly apologized out of habit.

Rose shrugged like she didn't know what I was talking about.

Chair cringed and said not to say that because, "See," Chair started explaining, "you can't hear the term 'grassy knoll' without thinking of blown-up heads and bloody laps. The word is ruined for my whole generation. No one relaxes or makes love on The Grassy Knoll. It's where snipers hide and shoot people. Every generation has their own references. We also can't think about the Bates Motel without a shower curtain, knife, and a scream."

"Yeah, me too," I eagerly agreed.

"Well, you've got to think about your own. Like Mom and apple pie, although that must be a pre–World War II reference because my mom never made an apple pie in her life. Anyway, now you've got me thinking that the little Yahoo girl's gonna snap and assassinate us. Can't you carve a working gun out of soap? Didn't they teach you anything clever in that place? No wonder the recidivism rate's so damn high."

"Sit down. We're gonna be just fine," Rose said.

We tried to sit there on that slope and not think about it, but every slap and clap had us on edge. We were a little too spooked by my use of the term "grassy knoll" to hang around much longer. So we packed up our picnic and bundled up the blankets and trudged all around the grass for a flat and muddy, un–grassy knoll–like place to settle.

We found what seemed to be the perfect spot near some low-profile hippies with skinny bare backs and a penchant for the blues, so we spread our Saturday afternoon selves out.

But it was an illusion. Tomfoolery. If Chair, Jean, and Rose hadn't been there, I wouldn't have believed it. But they were there, and we all looked at one another, frozen in stark-naked horror because the hippy bare backs morphed into lavender nylon, and once again we were sitting behind the *very same* Yahoo people as if we'd never even moved, and now the Yahoo girl was nuzzling, rolling, and suckling all over her Yahoo boy like a newborn kitten. . . .

I realized that THIS is what you get for hating a particular group so much: no matter where you move, God sends them to sit in front of you at the blues festival in corporate-purple Yahoo beach chairs. And don't think you can escape because wherever you go, *there they are.*

I also realized, as I quickly dumped my entire tumbler of Southern Comfort down my pie hole to get calm, that this is how rampant alcoholism gets started. Why do you suppose alcoholism is such a problem on Indian reservations? Because every time we drive through their reservations in our minivans, take pictures of their children, and ask if we can get five bucks off the price of a necklace, they have to resist the urge with all of their might to gouge our eyeballs out with concha belts and suck them past their lips like peeled grapes in the haunted house.

You see, my smoky old aunt Pad once hated black folks so much she wouldn't let my mom in her house once she married one. Aunt Pad retired to Florida with an invalid husband, a steady scrip for painkillers, and a full liquor cabinet. And over the years, her neighborhood turned so black, she couldn't even sell her condo to move out.

Ha ha, that's so funny she forgot to laugh.

I f I'd made three wishes on the shriveled monkey's paw, I'd have instantly understood the moral of my aunt Pad's tale.

Instead, I went to the hip lesbian café where they sold expensive peanut butter-and-jelly sandwiches and purple soda that made your tongue turn blue. They glamorized the blue-collar lifestyle, and for fun they cheated on girlfriends and wore used mechanic uniforms with men's names embroidered on them (the irony of it all), then called the place a truck stop. At night they often had art shows or spoken-word performances, and on the weekends, folksinging.

If the yupwazee couldn't possibly get enough of flowing wood-pulp clothing and innovative CD holders, then the lesbians turned the other way in disgust and couldn't get enough of nostalgic trailer parks, Saturday morning cartoons with morals, and Cap'n Crunch for dinner. All the things I loved.

All the sugar alone in one of their lunches added to the drama of lesbian breakups. They're invigorating and not for the faint of heart. Forget mud wrestling or monster-truck pulls. That's for pussies. If one of these girls was feeling down and thought she wanted to break up with you because the thrill was gone, you just had to hand her a bigger bowl of Lucky Charms, where the sugar content was higher. Yeah./It's all in the wrist, Sadie.

This truck stop café for make-believe blue-collar types started with "Vacuum Cleaner" Poontang, a real live Bearded Lady. Dina Poontang was part of the city's carpet-diving aristocracy, headed by Three-finger Gashly—now it's easy enough to figure out how Vacuum got her name, but I don't know whether Three-finger got this name because of the "hang loose" sign she used to say hello, or whether it was because of the special way she fucked.

She had a band called Tribe 9. The name is a play on the word *tribade*, which is all the frottaging that rugs do with each other after sniffing armpits and saying hello. They're in charge of all things rug and carpet.

I think they even bought a house, with wall-to-wall carpeting, of course, and I guess that would be the RUG PARLIAMENT, if so, but I can't be entirely sure.

Once when the café got robbed, they had a performance benefit so they could recoup their losses from the same girls

who sometimes couldn't even afford the retro sandwiches they served.

Rugs can be funny like that. Annie Sprinkle's houseboat in Sausalito burned up and she's probably still asking for donations to rebuild the porn-star lifestyle to which she's grown accustomed. Isn't anyone scratching her head asking, "Hmmm . . . own café? Own houseboat in Sausalito? . . ."

You're taught to watch out for big hair and giant tits, but don't be fooled by beards or flannel, either. Some girls have really got it down when it comes to convincing others to chip in for massages or pedicures. It's an art, this bartering without feeling like you're trading a cow for a handful of beans. My jeweler friend says you'd be surprised at how many women come into the store with smeared lipstick and a freshly milked man on their arm while they pick out another pair of gold earrings.

I can't say that about Three-finger Gashly, though. That girl has her own bicycle messenger company, "Gash Flash," and she got her training from riding around in the middle of the night getting ice cream and whatever else her girlfriends were suddenly craving. All of her butch friends made fun of her, calling her "gash in a flash" and that's where she got the name for her business. She puts out a newsletter for her business and calls it "The Laura Gashly Print."

For simplicity's sake, I call femme girls "cheerleaders," because a lot of them actually used to be cheerleaders in high school, so they already know how to keep the rest of us in our place and busy questioning our existence.

Anyway, now that I was back, I went to Vacuum's next café show. It was in a tiny place. Actually it was just a small alleyway in between buildings, with a counter at the end. People could only come in one right behind the other and pass their purchases back because it wasn't even as wide as a bus.

It could maybe hold fifteen people, but on this night, there were only ten little lesbians left in all of San Francisco: seven were in the audience, and three were performing.

To give it a sense of chaos, they only put four chairs out for their seven audience members. They were acting like people looking for housing in San Francisco, climbing over one another, kicking each other in the teeth, trying to grab a metal folding chair all their own.

I saw a milk crate right up front without a jacket on it, so I sat down, and a cheerleader member of the Lesbian Aristocracy in long candy-red hair and university-colored lipstick—she had so much jewelry hammered into her skull, and so many tattoos, so much Victorian ornamentation dripping off of her, she looked like a Fabergé egg with fangs—she sauntered up to me and freaked out because I clearly didn't know my place. Who did I think I was? This seat up front was automatically saved for someone else, *anyone else*, no matter what . . . yap, yap, yap, the Chihuahuas jumped in my head.

I knew who she was. University-lipstick girl was so famous there were numerous plaintive, wailing lesbian punk songs written about begging for the chance to writhe across broken beer bottles on bare stomachs to smell her dirty lingerie.

A girl sat up behind her and whispered in the university lipstick's ear, and the university-lipstick girl put her hands on her hips, set her high-heeled feet apart, and said, "Oh yeah—you're the lesbian O. J. Simpson who kidnapped your ex-girlfriend. Little kids tell each other the legend about how, to this day"—she paused and looked around for emphasis before pulling a penknife from her key chain and continuing—"they . . . *still* . . . can't . . . find . . . her.

"Furthermore"—she unfolded the penknife—"they say that when the sun goes down, if you look toward the ocean you can hear the wind crying for help in her name." University-lipstick girl brought the penknife, along with her entire key chain, to her teeth and started picking at them. That's when I noticed it was a Bikini Kat key chain. A place only open on Saturdays. "Did you know that?" She raised her eyebrows, sucked her teeth, and snapped the penknife shut. "I thought not. If I were you, I'd take a gander that you're not wanted here." University girl gestured widely around the room like a game-show girl. "Get out, Mrs. Hate Crime. We don't need your kind . . ."

And on and on she went like a player piano. I was seeing how the underground might not necessarily have the moral *high* ground.

So while I was busy hating the new people, I was busy being hated. You see, for I was seen as the lesbian O. J. Simpson for kidnapping my girlfriend. Lesbians are vegetarians studying to be therapists, so they're really into dredging up personal histories of abuse, and there I was, in the present tense, personifying lesbians' own internal blah blah blah, so they didn't want me to be a part of any more reindeer games.

Getting the hint, I went to the café down my block to hang out, a place called Fanari's. But Fanari's was changing, too. It was run by touchy, feely, sexy Argentinian men who listened to **TANGO** all day, and this inspired the rest of us to flirt endlessly and drink coffee for hours in the sun.

The once sparse bulletin board in the back, which had futons and Spanish lessons for sale, had now turned into a San Francisco Wailing Wall: layers upon layers of desperate and hopeful red and yellow flyers with untorn phone-number fringe asked for houses, apartments, rooms, places to sleep by fireplaces and offered up their children to do chores with dirty knees and cockney accents.

I looked around at Fanari's new customers, and most passed by with the carefully distracted confident look usually reserved for long elevator rides. Everyone was too important to stand in line, and no one was flirting with anyone. Soon enough, they'd be able to order coffee online or over the phone like movie tickets and never, ever have to stand in line again. Ever.

Would they ever flirt with anyone again? Oh, not in a harmless uncle and nephew in the sweaty barn sort of flirting, but the kind of flirting that actually leads to the

75.

confessional. What was all this? In a city whose mayors and political figures not only flirted with their **constituency,** but have been known to give sex for votes as well?

I stood there looking all around me with a tear in my eye like the Indian chief who cried because of all the litter.

Evil is not only in computer waste that contaminates the environment. Evil is not only in landlords who spend all day watering a lawn the size of a parking space and collecting six-figure rents. We also can't heave all the blame on a crummy coffee chain. There were many reasons that sex was covering itself up with a towel and running away from the city, and this was just one of them.

So there I was, hanging out in a sexless Fanari's café with my crayon, busily drawing up a new line of fake penises to start my fake-penis empire, out to catch all of my former penile glory—a glory I had nary a moment to enjoy before my last fall from grace.

But all of a sudden I remembered that HONDO had said there was a lull in dick art, because all the people who used to actually buy and use my fake penises had been evicted because they couldn't afford to live there any longer.

And these new folks were more focused on hot and throbbing bank accounts than on their private parts.

I knew that they wouldn't even use fake penises unless they could go online, make a phone call, schedule a meeting, input phone numbers, prevent wrinkles, or hold CDs with it. All of this change in a city that not only sleeps, but slept with all of its citizens, who used to pole-dance around parking meters for spare quarters.

I slammed my notepad down on the table because I was frustrated and didn't know what to do about it. Unfortunately I spilled my coffee on the local rag someone before had left at the table, the *San Francisco Bay Times*.

I ran to the sideboard to grab a pile of napkins to mop everything up, but when I came back, the cartoon in the paper seemed to be moving.

Looking all around me, everything seemed to be normal, so when I looked back I thought it was just my imagination and I continued mopping up. Just when I started to fold the paper up to toss it, I heard a muffled, "Hey, pssst . . ."

I opened the paper and the black-and-white cartoon started to move a little closer in the frame, and then she opened

her mouth and said
"It DOESN'T LOOK LIKE things ARE WORKING OUT FOR YOU, and—"
I CRUMPLED UP the soggy PAPER AND tossed it IN THE TRASH.
"ThANKS, Oscar
FLAM
I WAVED GOOD-BYE TO th
OWNER OF FANARI'S, AND hE CAM
FROM BehiNd THE COUNTER and gave me a HUG + KISS.
"Sometimes we Have to go away and start over again,"
he whispered in my ear.
PENIS IDEAS
I PULLED AWAY.
WHAT?
"I just SAid that it's good to see you BACK."
HE winked and WENt back behind the counter to pull a PINt glass DOWN FOR another coffee.

"yeah, okay."

I BACKED OUT of there and when I turned aRound I saw a billboard across THE street of the MARLboRo MAN in an SUV and he was waving TO ME.

FLAT BUTT? SUCK IN BED? NO PERSONALITY TO SPEAK OF? BUY THE NEW JAGUAR 4×4...

CLOSE-UP

That's WHEN I Realized it was time to pack it all in + do someThing ELSE. So I zipped my cRayon back in MY tROUSERS, and DECIDED to take most of my $10,000 LOAN and Put it toward a shiny BRand-New motoRcycle insTEAD, because if there's a CHANCE you may LoSE it all in the NEAR future, it's better to get the bike + RUN because HOUSES can't MOVE and You're NeVER homeless if you've got a bike. You can ALWAYS go somewhere ELSE + Do someTHING better without wondering if the BUS EVEN stops There.

Ask any GUy who's pushing a cart full of aluminum cans. If you ask Him whether there WAS a moment when he could've gone either WAY with A chunk of CASH, chances are He WENT with CoNVENTional wisdom + Bought SHoES for his kid and A job interview Suit instead of the BikE ...

Bikini Kat's™
ROADSIDE SHACK in SAN FRANSASSY, U.S.
Smart!
sassy!
stylish!™
"I got BIG IDEAS BIG Big HURRY."
©2001 FLOWER FRANKENSTEIN

DREAMS of CAKE & PARKING SPACES

I stopped into a little pink shop in the Castro district that was only open on Saturdays because the owner wanted to have a life: Bikini Kat's Roadside Shack. The walls were a healthy, internal organ pink, and silk-screened cat dolls with orange ponytails, riding cardboard motorcycles named Trixie, lined the walls. Clear plastic totem poles with fluorescent tubes lit up the place, and Bikini Kat mugs, key chains, soaps, penknives, and guns filled the internal organ pink store.

My wanting a new, preferably yellow bike and walking into a pink store was another one of those signs that I would be closer to the other white meat: mix those two colors, and you come up with the yellowish pink color of *uncooked* pork.

"Okeydokey, you comin' in, or what?" I heard a high giggle from what sounded like a little girl with a stuffed-up nose. *Une petite* brunette woman with bangs raised her head from behind the counter, and like most people who really make and do things—as opposed to just talking about them—she herself didn't look all done up and crazy in fake fur or sequins. She had normal bangs. Nothing pretentious or demanding like one of those art student girls.

La petite brunette woman opened a personal-pak of tissues, pulled one out, and held it up to her nose. "You're just in time!"

"I'm just in time for what?" I looked around suspiciously.

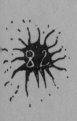

She blew her nose, smacked her hand on the counter, leaned toward me, and yelled, "Bikini Kat is giving away smart, sassy, and stylish rings so you can be smart, sassy, and stylish, too—just like Bikini Kat!"

Bikini Kat's gigantic and pink, and travels around the world on her motorcycle. At first her name was really Kitty Katty, but she changed it because she's going into show business.

Bikini Kat's sister, Kitty Glitter, lives in Hollywood, reads trashy magazines, and loves to gossip. Her hobbies are talking on the phone, karate chopping, inventing potions, watching horror movies, and singing heavy metal anthems. The Frankenstein/railroad-track scar on her forehead is from lots of plastic surgery—*lots*.

"Isn't she cool?" she whispered.

"The best," I whispered back in awe.

She tucked her personal-pak of tissues under the counter and asked, "And did you know that they invented tissues to take off ladies' makeup, but people used them to blow their noses instead?" I shook my head. She then presented me with a little yellow display box that had a drawing of three women looking at the rings on their hands, but with pasted Bikini Kat heads over the human heads. There was yellow foam that could hold seventy-two candy-machine rings. I had fifteen plastic-gold choices.

Tentatively, I reached my hand out for the one with a diamond the size of an ice cube. "For free?"

She pushed the box closer to me and I plucked my ice-cube diamond out and put it on my pinky finger. While I was admiring it, she said, "You know, I'm just not myself. This allergy medication makes me worse. I'm allergic to all the money blowing through the streets." It was true, there was an unimaginable amount of money in the Castro. She pulled another tissue out, sniffled, and wiped her nose. "All the fibers rubbing together, it's like pollen."

"Yeah, my sister's allergic to the color green. A mystic green Ford Explorer cut her off in the crosswalk and she keyed it with a deep groove along the side and ran away. She's been blowing her nose and wiping boogers on the

wall behind her bed ever since to keep from going insane. Nothing grosses me out anymore. Wipe your nose on my sleeve. Here—see if I care." I held up my sleeve and when she didn't take it, I switched the ring to my right hand so more people would notice it when I picked my own nose. "You know, you're right. I already feel smart and sassy, too. I don't usually talk about bodily functions." I lied. I talked about yeast infections whenever the opportunity presented itself.

"Here." She disappeared behind her counter again, and slapped a big deck of old, worn, pink tarot cards on the table. They were written and illustrated in marker, hastily colored in with crayons, and each card had the uneven edge of being cut by hand. "Shuffle the deck thoroughly and pick a card, any card."

I pulled off the top card, triumphantly smacked it down on the countertop, and waited for her to tell me what a great person I was.

She clapped her hands together and shouted, "Ah! Dreams of cake and parking spaces . . ."

There was a drawing of a square, three-layered cake, frosted like a cardboard box, and a spork had hacked away a good portion of the cake as if it had crashed into it.

On the top layer was a Transamerica Pyramid in powerful Mormon gold, with its Dracula collar, its weight crushing down on the layer cake. You knew that one little earthquake, and down it all goes.

Around the pyramid on the top layer were a bunch of little toy cars in cramped parking spaces, with one little car messing up all the frosting, still looking for a parking space.

On the second layer of the cake was a full parking garage, and on the bottom layer was a frosted highway heading east.

"Okay," she said. "Looks like you've picked the Seven of Sporks." She tapped her finger on the bottom of her lip and stared at the card, thinking . . . "Seven is a positive number, combining the practical and the possible. There are seven colors of the rainbow, and seven notes on the musical scale, and seven days of the week."

"Does that mean buying a new motorcycle is good?"

"And you know what sporks are, don't you? You get them at Kentucky Fried Chicken.

"The spork here is pointing east, and it means you're cutting through . . . The cake means that you want to have your cake and eat it, too, which could mean, hmm . . . maybe it means that you really work to have it all instead of giving in . . . and the square box cake means that you're thinking outside of the box. You're cutting away/putting yourself in a new head space. And the road: long, sharp, cutting and slicing onward through the landscape of cake. All in all, a good sign, I'd say."

"So I should buy the motorcycle, then?"

She snorted and shrugged. "Sure, I guess." She absently looked out the window, and passersby were trying in vain to grab at money blowing all around them as if they were in a game-show booth with air jets, but they caught nothing; you have to slather your body in a special, expensive lotion made by the Japanese that only the very special people who park on sidewalks can buy.

Her focus suddenly narrowed and settled on me as she leaned forward, lowered her voice, and pointed at me with each syllable. "But it depends. There's a decidedly yellow cast to this reading, in that there's a downside to this as well that you'll have to be cautious of.

"If you're not careful, because the number seven is also tricky, things could also turn bad. You've got to listen with your heart, a clear mind, and be realistic. Seven days of the week and the seven musical notes on the scale will lead you to your seven colors of the rainbow. You must be careful, for if you get out of balance, and bad characteristics are allowed to come out and override compassion, you're allowing selfishness to rule. And no matter how noble your original intent, secret fears and worries will cast despondent shadows over the brightest events."

I stared at her for a minute with a dumb look of horror on my face because I hated ominous warnings like these. It wasn't fair. How was I supposed to know when I was out of balance? There was no scale. No narrator. No oracle. No gallery dealer to exploit me and supply me with drugs and art supplies. No audience to yell out what's around the corner.

You never find out if you're doing the right thing until it's all over, and the dust has settled around your retirement home. If you're alone playing horsie with your golf clubs and your grown kids never call you, you've still got one last deathbed chance to make amends. Or when you break your hip.

Yeah, it seems like you never know if what you did was right until it's too late. And in the face of her assured optimism, I couldn't disappoint her waiting eyes by saying nothing. I lowered my voice dramatically, nodded profoundly, and spoke slowly about her sober warning about a loss of compassion leading to selfishness, "Aha! I get it. You're saying that I should get the motorcycle but *drive carefully*, then."

"Okay, well . . ." She dropped her gaze on the table and looked back up at me as if she hadn't noticed at first that I was a special child who had to take special buses to school. She shook her head and continued in a louder, slower manner that told me quickly, before dust settling around any retirement home, that I'd *already* done the wrong thing by following up with a question about a new motorcycle, "Hmmm . . . okay, well . . . I see. . . ." She stammered for my level. "But a *yellowing* motorcycle would be more real and less about prettiness for show." She stopped, gently took my hand, and looked at me. "Do you understand?" I nodded my head, and in case I couldn't read her lips, she made circles around the side of her head and motioned as she spoke. "A yellowing motorcycle will keep you riding across frosted highways and give you a slicing-through-the-landscape-of-a-cake kind of modest life that you can eat, too."

And speaking of eating, then we had bright orange cheese crackers and apple juice and talked.

And that's how I met Flower Frankenstein, *une petite* woman with unpretentious bangs. She said that with a name like that, most people looked for a tall transvestite. "A bad perm," she later told me when I asked her how she got the name Flower. Like a chrysanthemum.

She blew her nose and blew my mind. I didn't fully understand, but I had a six-pack desire for truth, and there it was in the Seven of Sporks tarot card. Take away the "s" on either side and you've got pork. If I'd known what I know now, I'd have known that I was also that much closer to the other white meat/or as they say in Canada: *C'est l'autre viande blanche.*

Now her shop's not even open on Saturdays anymore because all of her customers had to leave town, so if you go to San Francisco, you won't find her. Such nonstop fun is over.

I left Flower's and just in case I needed a bigger smack upside the head to get me to leave the city, a gold-plated, jewel-encrusted Louis XIV mobile the size of a loft barged through and ran over a few children to cut me off to make a turn. But his Firestone tires exploded and he got hit by a taxi running a red light. I should've been the one who got hit. And that's when I realized that I'd better watch out because now there could be a falling chrysanthemum pot with my name on it.

The taxi was crushed up like a half-eaten TV dinner, and the Arabian taxi driver was trapped inside, with his right arm casually draped around his neck like a pashmina scarf, screaming frantically that he couldn't feel anything below his chin.

The Louis XIV mobile driver slid down a thick rope tied to his steering wheel just like he practiced it in gym class, and pulled the Maxipad phone off the side of his face just long enough to dial 911. He was a lucky man, and not just because he could afford so much; his mobile merely had blown-out tires, and he could barely contain a smile as he patted his Fred Flintstone stomach, waved his arms, and told the gawking crowd that he was just fine.

But he's the one they'd wanted to see dead. In the light of day, all the people were forced to use their mob mentality for good and collectively suppress the urge to reenact the old Elizabeth Taylor film where they'd chase him up a classically steep San Francisco hill, surround him, stomp him like a wooly mammoth, and eat him.

The taxi driver sat motionless with his right arm still wrapped fashionably around his neck. He started to cry.

Yes, I figured this definitely was a sign, so in the morning I gave my bike to the first furry middle-aged guy I saw with a shopping cart riffling through the trash for recyclables. He had bright blue eyes, rough fat hands, and a huge woodsman's beard. He said he hadn't ridden since he was sixteen, but he did just fine riding it up and down the street. I went back inside, riffled through my kitchen junk drawer for the pink slip, signed it over. For the "buyer's" address, he put down his brother's in Mendocino. I said, "Well, where do you get your welfare check sent?" but he said he didn't want to be a welfare king, corrupted by all that money: he wanted to remain a simple man, and I nodded and understood.

So I gave him a five-dollar helmet I got at Goodwill, a handful of tools, the Chilton manual, some old insurance and registration papers in case he needed extra time changing things over, and waved good-bye. He left his shopping cart in front of one of the places where the Chihuahuas lived and I fantasized that they'd be scampering around like barking rats and the sound would cause the cart to roll over and crush them to death. Or at least it would inspire them to scamper off to freedom, away to the part of Mexico where, every Sunday, they maniacally stab Chihuahuas with toothpicks like Karen Black in *Trilogy of Terror*, and eat them up.

I was hoping that maybe I'd helped to change this man's life, somebody's life anyway, given him a new freedom.

I ran into him later when he was leaning against the wall across the street with his eyes fluttering back into his head like when you've got a Q-Tip in your ear, and he focused on me long enough to thank me. All of his teeth were now gone. He said he got fifty bucks for my bike.

So I optimistically went to Munroe Motors over on Valencia Street. All the mechanics there were sexy because they knew how to ride fast and fix things, which is a little like having your hands held over your head while being kissed. I asked the pink salesman with sweat stains under his armpits if they had any yellowing bikes. No, he told me regrettably, they only had orange ones.

Disappointed, I left and got myself a cheap white lipstick at the drugstore for a dollar. It was fun, like buying a lottery ticket, except you can't smear a lottery ticket all over your lips. Suddenly feeling lucky, I walked back to Munroe Motors and said, "Hey, Mister Salesman, I just wanted to say that if you come across a *yellowing* motorcycle, give me a call." I handed him my number written down on the receipt from my white lipstick.

"Wait." He snapped his clammy fingers as if remembering why he was alive. "Come with me." The pink motorcycle salesman lit up because now he'd be able to afford a goose for Christmas and a glass eye for his dog. "This one sat in the front window too long and faded to a . . ."

". . . yellowing bike!" What a miracle! I bought myself the yellowing bike. I loved that bike so much, I used to just brush my lips and teeth against my rubber-cushioned handlebars at stoplights, half-expecting someone to add me to the list of urban myths, like baby-sitters who bring over dingo dogs to eat the children if the microwave isn't big enough; or instances of ringing cell phones trapped up people's rectums in emergency rooms.

I made the mistake of calling up HONDO to tell him about my new bike: "What *yellowing* bike?" he spat.

"Oh yeah, I decided not to go back into business, but to buy a yellowing bike instead," I explained.

"No! No! No! I was investing in your *business*!"

"What? Well, I thought I'd just pay you back."

"What do you think I am? An ATM on Rollerblades? I want my money now, with interest! Oh, oh, oh—and not pussy mutual fund interest! No, ma'am. What I would have made if I'd invested in Yahoo! stock." He pulled out a calculator; I could hear him jabbing and stabbing at the little keys.

"But you didn't invest in Yahoo! stock. I remember you thinking that it's a bad risk to put so much into computer stocks because you said it's all speculation and isn't based on logic. Like how the peppy dork who started Amazon.com is a multibillionaire while the company has yet to make a profit. I remember you saying that. I don't really think you would've bought Yahoo! stock. I think you would've bought more khaki pants with the $10,000 if you ask me—and while they flatter your backside and you look handsome in them, khakis tend to depreciate in value once you remove the tags."

"If I hadn't given you that money, I would have put it all in Yahoo!, missy, and that's the point." It sounded like he hurled his calculator across the room.

"Did you just hurl your calculator across the room?" I asked.

"Yes. I don't need it because I already know you owe me an awful lot. It went up 390 percent last week. How am I supposed to be a millionaire by forty-five with people like you sucking me dry? You waste my time, my money, now—"

"Yeah, well, Mister Control Man, you can't control everything, you know. Some people do soul-searching, but ever since I got out of jail, I've been evaluating my phone book and you all suck. I've been going through it and there's just no one I wanna talk to anymore. So do you know what I'm gonna do? Huh? I'm gonna get a new phone book . . . and a *pen!*" And then I cursed him because he really could control everything forever, as white educated men who don't think about philosophy too much have been controlling things for as long as anybody's

herstory, theirstory, history could remember. But no one was really paying attention to history. It was just quietly becoming the thirty-second flavor.

"I want you out of that shack so I can sell it to loft developers! Do you hear, you goddamned—?" He yelled and slammed the phone down on himself.

And speaking of history, I'd never cursed HONDO before—not in an unloving, unappreciative tone, anyway. Things were different forever. And not in the kind of way that made me want to throw my angora beret in the air and twirl around. No. The kind of way that made me want to chase him up a classically steep San Francisco hill, surround him, stomp him like a wooly mammoth, and eat him.

We know where Rick James is . . . but where's California, where's Teena Marie, and where's the underground that's gonna give us all new social security numbers and phony credit ratings? Without them, most of us are supremely fucked. *Unless* you've got a reason to believe in inheritance: pray that your folks are the ones who thought social activism was cute, protested only during study hall, and went ahead and got their business and law degrees in spite of the fact that all that the world needed was love, because then you're the heirs who're gonna get your houses after all and miss all this mess.

I'd been holding on to my Beatrix Potter lifestyle by the skin of my teeth, and now I was losing ground. By and by, my lights, water, power, and gas were shut off. I couldn't see what I was doing and I was tripping over everything. Sure, the glasses were probably rinsed out with urine and the plates scrubbed down with roach carcasses, but the light was dim. And as Tennessee Williams has shown us time and time again, dim lighting is everything. A 40-watt bulb shaves years off and dirt disappears. Why, you don't ever have to do the dishes again. Just wipe the lipstick off the rims.

Look at me now. America's back in the eighties and so am I. The eighties, back before Goth was called "Goth" and us serious art students didn't need black lipstick to heal our broken, vitamin C–deficient lips because we *were* black lipstick and it was labeled "Oppression" for a dollar ninety-nine. Oh oh oh baby, you should've been there when we lubricated our souls with Jean-Michel Basquiat's heroin-fringed optimism. Ha! Would you like paper or plastic, sir? Say it enough times and the roomful of flax will be spun into gold.

Back then the whole world seemed to be there for our taking, and even I stepped over homeless people, thinking that all they had to do was pick themselves up by the bootstraps—like those of us who could pass in and out through Ebonics or French like beaded curtains. Long before our time, we were all turning into boring white, post–WWII Republican businessmen who got free education and houses with 2 percent down, but after that, yelled, "We the people blame the victim! No more government intervention!"

Most everything was black in the eighties . . . halogen lights, kitchen Formica, souls, and even roses were black. Banks gave us credit cards like after-dinner mints, so now my credit report is the color of an era, the color of Reagan's hair.

I don't trust anyone *under* fifty because I'm part of the "I Was Just Pettin' It, George" generation, and if life were Vietnam and a land mine had just blown off your leg, we really *would* go on without you. If you want to die without bedsores, you'd better have a separate retirement account just for the tips alone. We won't smile for free. Either that or keep on going to that gym and try to make it to the bathroom on your own as long as possible. Knowing my people, I'd hide a couple of cyanide tablets in your class ring if I were you and give euthanasia the old college try.

If you don't believe me, remember we're the ones who had ATM machines at Woodstock '99 and rioted over $4 water and $10 burritos. That's our excuse. But we would've rioted even if the water and burritos were free, *because* they were free. We just get so bored.

Over tea, Flower had said, "It's almost like technology is our Vietnam War. We're losing so many people. They're becoming zombies. That disease where you can't click anymore—what is it?—carpal tunnel. And they're all shell-shocked from looking at screens all day long and when they get home from work and when they see a movie on the weekends. We're facing a big wall. We don't have a cause. Everyone's too pacified to fight.

"What'll all the bums be saying in the future? 'I was in World War II' . . . 'I was in the Vietnam War' . . . 'I was in the war on drugs.' "

It was time to leave San Francisco. The signs were as potent as a director hooking me offstage with a cane.

And that last night in the flamboyant City of Second Chances, I had a dream, a scary dream. The scariest kind of all. Not about jail, about being forced to behave in French restaurants, or about growing old with no health insurance and the inability to scream. But the nightmares and stories we used to tell each other in the clubhouse when I was a kid in West Virginia and we'd lay our heads in somebody's scary lap and they'd massage the terrifying stories into our temples forever with little circles . . .

. . . There was the one about the man with the golden arm, come back from the grave to get his arm back. The one you stole and hid under your pillow so you'd be richer than your wildest dreams and then no one could ever tell you not to eat chocolate mint chip ice cream for breakfast . . .

But this was the one where I'd spent the hot dog money on a toy, got some hot dog buns with the change, went to the graveyard and CUT OFF the long-dead friendly old janitor's FINGERS. I gave them to Mom so I wouldn't get in trouble for coming home without supper.

That was back in the days before anything was SEALED/BACK in the days when TRICHINOSIS was cking. And you could pretty much come home with a fistful of ground pork in your pocket, pick the hair off, and spit on it for luck BEFORE YOU FRIED it up in A PAN.

So my mom and sister put the JANITOR'S FINGERS in the HOT DOG buns and ate them with mustard and ketchup.

I went to sleep, BUT in the middle of the night I heard a light RAPPING on my bedroom door, and a DISTANT, finny wail from the other side, like AN OLD PHONE CALL FROM A FARAWAY LAND. I ALSO HEARD MY NAME

I TRIED TO Bite my tongue into Reality so I could fall asleep again. And just as I convinced myself that it was **Nothing**, **Nothing** at all, the RAPPing Came again, only this time it sounded like a scraping squishiness thudding at the door. **BONE-LIKE** the bones and bloody meat of what's left of an old man's hands.

Like A PORK NECK

¿¿¿ Mr. Janitor Man? ??? MY VOICE QUAVERED AT SUCH a high pitch, dogs as far away as CANADA could hear me. I was SO afraid, I DROPPED MY hAND UNDER MY BED AS I DID EVERY NIGHT, TO SEE if my dog, Mittens, would lick the PALM. SHE DID. OR AT lEAST I thought it was my dog, BECAUSE AT THAT moment ----

THE UNSOPHISTICATED SALT lick on my palm TURNED INTO A ~~SATANIC~~ ~~tongue PROBE into~~ the CROtch of a couple of my fingers, right here where this thin flap of skin is, see? And I FlinchED my hAND bAck.

~~I~~ WAS Afraid to look under the BED. And just THEN, I heard something ~~CORPSE~~-HEAVY and dull BEING SLOWLY DRAGGED BACK And forth in front of MY BEdroom DOOR to TAUNT me. At times it PAUSED to relish this SPECIAL KiND of MOMENT that would HAUNT THiS little girl FoR YEArs UNTiL HER own KNEECAPS WOULD turn To powder and by then her laugh lines WOULD BE so deep, she could tuck SPAre CHANGE into them like sofa cushions.

~~B~~UT For NOW, SOMETHiNG with a tongue UndeR my bed and thAT POUNDING AT the DOOR MADE me MUTE with ripped-BACK fingernail FEAR WHILE MY HOWLING OLD JANitoR man WAS pawing at the DOOR with The Wet stumps thAT USED to TURN The PAGES iN Bedtime STORIES, SHUCK PEAS, switch the CHANNEL/WET stumps that'd WAVED to THE mailman, shoveled the ↗

↗ DRiVEWAY, pulled the voting levers for presidents, helped the UPS drivers hold pencils when their CARPAL tunnel flared up. / And there, there THEY WERE, THUDDING AGAINST the DOOR like Little xylophoNE mallets, asking WHEre his fingers WERE, and I WAS too SCARED to even Exhale, much less explain anything and EVERYTHING.

I MOVED TO RUN UNDER THIS THICK NIghtmare WAterfall, TO MAKE IT TO THE WINDOW and ESCAPE, but I felt SOMETHING TEARING AT my NIGHTiE HEM, slowing me down. I WHIPPED MY HEad AROUND and EXPECTED TO SEE my jANiTOR MAN grabbing AT ME WITH his STRONG PALMS, his mouth open, vying for a SPECIAL place in my childhood Nightmares with his teeth CLAMPED DOWN ON My NightiE, the SLIME FROM his LipLess mouth DROPPING like PANCAKE BATTER onto a grill, burning "Tsssss!" through the HARdWOOd floor. But instead it WAS A HOUND FROM HELL, A ROTTING chihuahua with CHUNKS of flesh plopping off his rib cage like chicken Nuggets and jiggling oN THE Floor LIKE STRAWBERRY JELL-O.

My FINGERLESS jANitor man's CORPSE Was no Longer THUDDING its STUMPS AGAinST MY BEdRooM dooR, FoR he WAS now inside my bedRoom with me. I tripped oVER my NEW toy, LITERALLY/SYMBOLICALLY/SPIRItually, and after I REACHED out foR the winDow LEdge to Break my fall, I turned to face him.

HE STOOD THERE WITH DRIED MUd and Hay AND CRUShed cigarette butts all OVER His FACE, WitH WORMS SQUIRMING at tHE Edge of His Rotting eye Sockets like SEXY DICTATORS Belly DANcing ON BALConies OVER tHE TOWN SQUARE. It WAS oBViOUS that they WRitHED foR FREEDOM. They sHook their little WORM Fists FROM tHE Edge OF HiS EYE SOCKET BALConies and opENEd THEiR miniATURE WORM MoutHS to CRy foR REVENGE! SHRIEK foR JUSTICE! AND CATERWAUL FoR my SCALP.

Slowly UNHinging his jAw to SPEAK,

EXTRA WORMS tumbled FROM his
CRACKED and ROTTiNG LiPS LiKE children
FALLiNG OUT of Amusement PARK Rides.
He coughed, clearing some
jammed WORMS FROM his throAt,
bringing THEM BACK UP as ground
meat to RE-SWALLOW, and in A
WATERY guttURAL ECHO, simply
TOLD ME, "It's time for us to have
a creepy little chat," and he
DEMANDED his FiNGERS BACK.
"Give 'em back, or else..."

I STUTTeReD, "B-b-but you can't
have them back./We ate th-th-them."

I STILL COULDN'T BREATHE, AND
THANK GOD I DIDN'T HAVE TO INHALE
THE ROTTING AROMA OF A MAN WHO'S EITHER

DEAD

OR HAS BEEN CAMPING ALL SUMMER.

I could only grip the window ledge and frantically shake my HEAD and hope to convey with my eyes how TRULY SORRY I WAS, and COULD I HAVE A QUARTER?

Mr. Janitor man coughed and asked me in that low, gravelly whisper HE had EVEN BACK WHEN I was a little girl, "Feel lucky, kid?" He held up his jAGGED palms. "If I had 'EM, How many fingers Would I BE HOLDING UP, HUH? Is it five fingers or SIX? C'mon, don't be sHy..." He WAVED his palm stumps at me to hurry me up in an almost loving way, like a coughing uncle with emphysema who plays that trick where he pretends his thumbs can come apart.

And I guessed WRONG by SAYING SEVEN, but I don't think I ever REALLY HAD a chance Anyway, BeCause that kind of game's BEEN RIGGED SINCE The BEGinNING of TiME, AND so he Held up ONE fingerless HAND OVER his head and SAID, Hallelujah, I'm in the spirit now

When he was done doing the jig and waving his ARMS in the air, HE BENT DOWN, RESTED HIS WRIST Bones on his KNEES, AND LEANED forward to tell me, "Well now, bad little girl, don't look so surprised. You gone and screwed up. You were supposed to do better. AW, heck, why'd you think I sent your mama those twenty-dollar bills in the first place? You were such a cute little girl then. While all them other kids was RUNNin' around with egg yolk 'n snot on their collars, your mama brought you to school so CLEAN, with all the NAPS combed outa your hair, even though she got all your new school clothes at Goodwill before they got all the extra-fancy stuff like now. Now you jes' a secondhand ho...."

HE gestured AT THE MESS THAT WAS ME WITH HIS STUMPS and shook His HEAD SADLY. "You all grown up and you ain't so clean no more. Why look at yourself, girl. You're a dirty, NAStY OLD thing now, even though all your things are New. Too Damn dirty inside.

"And then you GONE and Done somethin' stupid. You done stole my fingers... Nah, you didn't turn out right at all. NOT AT ALL. You weren't so special after all. Just gone and messed up like the Rest of us. A little worse, even?"

He shook his head and stood upright. "But don't ~~XXX~~ WORRY; you get yourself a little consolation PRIZE jes' for showin' up and PLAYin' at the whole thing in the FIRST place." HE REACHED INSIDE HIS JACKET WITH HIS PALM STUMP AND POKED AROUND, AND OUT IT CAME WITH A STUFFED **Bikini Kat** DOLL impaled ON HIS JAGGED WRIST BONE. "FOR YOU." HE smiled as HE FLICKED THE DOLL OFF ON THE SIDE OF MY FACE like a PIECE of MEAT off a FORK.

AND HIS FINGERLESS HAND POINTED A LONG ACCUSATORY STUMP AT ME AND LEANED FORWARD EVEN CLOSER TO WHISPER, "GIRLY, YOU remember this one thing: no one escapes unscathed when it comes to MEAT, AND the search FOR it will lead you Down a Baaaad, bad path.... You'll be followed by the Hounds of hell... the SOUNDS of BARKING Chihuahuas FOREVER. THEY will scream at you, and SCARE You EVERY DAY UNTIL YOU DIE! DIE! ~~DIE~~ ! OH, YES, THERE'S NO TELLIN' HOW LONG BEFORE THEY BURROW INTO YOUR DREAMS, DIG UP YOUR FLOWERS... GNAW AT YOUR HOPES, AND PISS ON YOUR PROM DRESS. WHATEVER LOOKS NICE AND SWEET IS GONNA BE TURNED INTO SOMETHING AWFUL... REAL, REAL BAD."

I STILL HEARD SOMETHING CORPSE-HEAVY AND DULL BEING SLOWLY DRAGGED BACK and FORTH IN FRONT of MY BEDROOM DOOR, OCCASIONALLY PAUSING FOR EMPHASIS. WHAT...

WAS THE SOUND? I SUDDENLY PANICKED—
WHERE WAS MITTENS? "W-W-W-WHAT HAVE
YOU DONE WITH MY PUPPY?" MY LITTLE VOICE CRACKED
OUT INTO THE DARKNESS IN AN EERIE FALSETTO
USUALLY RESERVED FOR CHOIRBOYS SINGING IN
EMPTY PUBLIC BATHROOMS, WHERE THE ACOUSTICS
ARE SUPERB.

THE EVIL CHIHUAHUA TOSSED HIS HEAD BACK AND CACKLED.

MR. JANITOR MAN DIDN'T ANSWER ME, JUST SHRUGGED
AND WIPED AT A DECAYING NOSTRIL WITH HIS STUMP,
WHERE A WORM TWISTED FREE, THEN THUDDED QUIETLY
TO THE FLOOR. IT DELICATELY SQUIRMED FOR PURCHASE,
AND STARTED TO SLINK TOWARD JANITOR MAN'S SHOE
LIKE A BATTERED WIFE GOING BACK FOR MORE, BUT
MR. JANITOR MAN JUST TURNED ON HIS HEEL AND
WALKED OUT THE DOOR, LEAVING ME ALONE WITH
THE WORM AND YEARS OF BONE-CHILLING SOUNDS OF
SOMETHING STILL BEING SLOWLY DRAGGED ACROSS THE
PAST AND PRESENT HARDWOOD FLOORS OF MY LIFE, JUST
BEYOND MY BEDROOM DOOR, AND OUT TO A FUTURE THAT SURPRISINGLY
SMELLED LIKE STRAWBERRY JELL-O AND SO I MANAGED TO CONVINCE
MYSELF THAT THE DRAGGING, SCRAPING SOUND ON THAT NIGHT WAS ONLY A
BIG, HEAVY BAG OF BLOODCURDLING FLOUR.

IT DID TAKE ME A LONG TIME TO FIGURE OUT WHAT
THE DRAGGING, SCRAPING SOUND ACTUALLY WAS. BUT
MORE ABOUT THAT LATER, BECAUSE IT WAS BAD ENOUGH
THAT I WOKE UP THAT MORNING CLUTCHING A BIKINI
KAT DOLL IN MY BED WITH A BLOODY, RAGGED HOLE
IN HER BACK. INSERT SCREAM HERE

Uh oh, Bikini Kat™!
oh my stomach
insert stump here
Hello my name is
Hi.
pep
I help

Stop with pop!

you are on page 113 of this book!

Draw Pop

That same ruthless morning I also realized that if I went with the California bad-energy avalanche that was happening, I was truly no longer meant to be here. But leaving is a great big deal because I felt like there's no better life outside of San Francisco and so I leave with two feelings: sad that I'm leaving behind something that could be so great, but isn't; and again, I had no idea what I was going toward.

It would've been nice to ride out to the desert with a squinty-eyed sense of Linda Hamilton *Terminator* purpose. She was so focused because she was pregnant with a kid who was actually going to save the world, instead of aiding in its demise. I had no purpose. I still can't even figure out whether to shop at a corporation to save a dollar or make the independent guy who owns Amoeba Records even richer.

It's tough to always do the right thing, like avoid chain stores at least one day a week. The good thing about corporate chain stores is that you can take back just about anything within thirty days and get your money back, whereas some independent shopkeepers might suddenly pretend they didn't speak English.

Bikini Kat measure things

I've used corporate bookstores and electronics stores as kinds of lending libraries. I might buy an answering machine or a camera to get me through a pinch and take it back later.

But some independent places make the owners millionaires and they underpay their employees if they can. And doesn't a public corporation spread the wealth around just a little more equitably with all the shareholders? Safeway supermarkets have their employees say "Thank you" and ask if you need help with your groceries, and their cashiers get union wages.

You go to Rainbow, the big San Francisco health food store, and it's supposed to be a loving organic world co-op where the employees get percentages of the profits. But for all the health food in that place, the anemic employees look annoyed. No policies make them say "Thank you, can I help you with your bags?" so they won't, unless they damn well feel like it. And you're already asking for too much because you not only pay more, but you've got to bag your own groceries.

Everything's so expensive. I'm amazed that a small armful of non-death chemical-free food costs so much. I'm always asking the cashier to take things back.

Only the elite can afford healthy, non-death-provoking food without irradiation, or no growth hormones, or free-range chicken that hasn't been tossed around like a volleyball by underpaid workers whose husbands and pregnant wives are out in the fields getting sprayed by pesticides for the tomatoes and grapes for the rest of us to buy on sale.

There could be more solidarity in shopping, dying, eating, getting paid real money, and waiting in line for bleached and spoiled meat along with the rest of the masses at Food Lion.

Life is full of contraindications.

I don't know how long I just lay there in bed waiting for a crack of lightning, flickering sunshine, or even a fart from a homeless person outside my window, waiting for some kind of sign, but it must've been a long time because my neck popped like bubble wrap when I turned to look out the window. The outside world didn't know. Now was the time to focus inward and listen to my body, and the popping sounds in my neck clarified for me that I had the choice between getting out now or staying in San Francisco, where I'm the lesbian O. J. Simpson; my relationship with HONDO has become litigious; and my life as an artist in

San Francisco has been reduced to "fill in the blank." The only thing in the right place in my life was the motorcycle between my legs.

The other choice was dropping that clutch through all five gears and leaving it in its highest gear for twenty hours.

Like cornering the last few peas onto my fork at the finish of a meal, my thoughts came simply and clearly, for there was only one math question left to answer: if I drove in fifth gear for twenty hours, how far away *would* I be?

Hurriedly, I packed up a few things, put on my unfinished "Flaming Iguanas" gang jacket that said F.I.A.M., and skipped to Goodwill to pick up some new gear to wear on my bike. All for under ten bucks, I strapped on a cracked riot gear helmet; picked up some nice vinyl gloves with questionable stains on just a few fingers; and slipped on a pair of barely scratched swimming goggles. The goggles were to protect my eyes while I got a face tan that would make me age prematurely. I was hoping to tan my face enough to make my teeth look white, and blend in the scars from the botched amateur electrolysis job I gave myself when I was in prison.

I closed the door behind me, turned the house keys in the lock, and decided to just leave them dangling in the door, like a metal ponytail. I loved my western sunset good-byes—the kind where you flicked your last cigarette into the horizon and mounted your bike like a UPS driver mounting the stairs or a receptionist.

So I flung my right leg over the seat, flicked up the kickstand, and well, there aren't too many bikes out there for shorter folks, and my yellowing bike is so big, I tiptoe when straddling it. What happened was I lost my footing on the cat litter on the sidewalk I had put down to soak up the oil from my last bike. My bike fell on my ankle before I could move it out of the way, and I was pinned to the ground. The pain was so intense, those Canadian dogs could even hear this scream, too.

And in spite of what I told people then, I really couldn't pick the bike back up with my lower lips. At least not at that point in my life. Before nearly passing out, I had to frantically wave down three passing homeless guys.

I survived, of course, but to this day, I still have a weird hard knot above my ankle, like a slice of hard-boiled egg that aliens wedged under my skin when I wasn't looking

When I'm lonely and insane, I ask it for advice and talk to *it*. It lives.

And so with my sidekick knot above my superhero ankle, I left my doubt in San Francisco and took off for a frosted highway heading east forever, a salmon against the steady flow of traffic of overpriced cars. Again facing the g-force winds of my future with my flab flying all behind me, pulling the skin from my face, I looked like a flying squirrel as I squinted into the sun with my unpregnant purpose.

All that was left that day in the Castro were disillusioned transplants from the East Coast looking for peace of mind and parking spaces like zombies on that Tuesday afternoon/a day that never held a lot of promise for anyone the way a Monday or Friday can. That's why Tuesday's the prettiest-sounding day of the week.

didn't quite make it twenty hours on the new yellowing bike. I was leaning so far forward on my hand, it fell asleep after eighteen hours. I pushed on into the desert so I'd at least feel like I was getting somewhere. Eventually I got carpal tunnel like a UPS driver and I couldn't shift too well since I couldn't feel my fingers, and my knees got all cramped up. I didn't like my yellowing upright bike. It looked all retro and cool, but I'm just going to have to come to terms with the fact that I'm never going to be cool. Cool is like high heels, uncomfortable because it's always a balancing act.

For me, cool always weighs heavily on the ugly or dark side. Consider: bulimic fashion models with false teeth, because years of vomiting stomach acid have rotted the original set. Face-lifts that involve yanking skin off your skull, like a chicken breast, and having it pulled tightly back, stapled back to your skull, and held in place with a screw. I am the false teeth. I am the skull staples. And I'm okay with that because I can only get worse when I'm actually rotting.

According to the more direct road signs, the road would veer off into two directions up ahead a little ways. I guess that's why I stopped behind the old vegetable stand at the

side of the road to pee, so I'd have a chance to buy a little time and figure out what next.

It took me a long time to do my pants back up because my left hand was floppy, and I couldn't move it.

I went inside the dilapidated stand and looked through rusty tomato-paste cans for something interesting. What if I found something valuable? I found cans full of nails, razor blades, paper clips, and other miscellaneous hardware for a roadside stand—broken and melted muddy crayons, staples, and flattened paint brushes. Oh, and cans full of forks. About six big cans full of forks. They were thin, tinny, and bent, but they weren't rusty: aluminum. And I hear that traces of aluminum may cause Alzheimer's.

Of course I took all these forks as a sign regarding the impending fork in the road.

Pulling one of the forks out of a can, I walked to a flat patch of sand and dropped to my knees. I stuck the fork in the side of my mouth, bit down on one of the tines, then yanked the fork down so it would be bent out like a hitchhiker's thumb. When I tossed the fork high up into the air and it dropped into the soft sand, the tine was leaning to the left. To the left, just like my political views and the

120

knot on my left leg, so I figured left was the way to go when I came to the fork in the road.

I stood up, and when I wiped the sand off my knees, I noticed my knees were pretty filthy with dead bug guts from riding. There was also some big, crusty, yellow-green bug smear on my left leg just in case I wasn't convinced. Left leg. Dead left hand. Verify, testify. Miracles do happen every day.

I got back on my bike feeling pretty sure of myself, and when I got to the fork in the road, there was my own Chanticleer sign in the shape of meat that said PORK IN THE ROAD, pointing left, and in smaller lettering below the PORK IN THE ROAD advertisement, a sign in the shape of a mushroom cloud that had written on it AREA 54 ～～... ...～6 MI/FOOD/GAS/LOVE with a crudely painted bra underneath, and a scribbled note on the back of a little square of chipboard that read: *Turn right at the black mailbox.*

Out on the still horizon, in the direction I was heading, there was a huge plume of smoke. For a second, it looked like an atomic mushroom cloud, but it was just an illusion, the way a cloud in the sky was up behind the billowing

smoke. How strange, I thought. Maybe this would constitute a bad sign. Still, I was too curious to turn away.

I followed the hand-painted signs that kept on appearing whenever there was a turn, and after a handful of miles, I ended up at a rickety old white ranch with a patch of green sod in front. I turned in at the black mailbox like the note said to do. Goats with ten-foot horns chased me as I rode up the gravel driveway that wound around the back of the main house. I could smell the barbecue and there were four or five eighteen-wheelers parked in this makeshift parking lot.

Now let me make known my feelings about pork. I don't like it and it smells like fat and greedy foster-parent sweat—the sweat of a bad Wonder bread and head-cheese diet on nasty vinyl in the summertime. But by then, I was hungrier than I've ever been for something that I've never tasted.

I walked from the driveway to the little counter and no one was there. There was a white plastic trellis right next to the counter, with a hole in it that you walked through to get to the back of the house. The house itself looked as if it had some kind of courtyard in the middle, with a small in-ground pool where a few truckers with permanent barbecue-sauce stains on their shirts were stretched out in chaise longues, taking naps in the sun.

I reached out and rang a big "come-and-get-it" triangle.

"Hold your horses, now!" A raspy woman's voice that must've once been tailor-made for a perfume commercial, bellowed from what looked to have been the goat shed at one time. She pushed open the screen door of the shed with a big platter covered in tinfoil and squinted at me in the bright daylight. "Good night! You're a little early, aren't you?" She was tiny. Tiny, tiny, like drag queens who give lipstick kisses on the mouth. This is how tiny she was.

She had a red, moth eaten ostrich feather boa around her neck and a cigarette in her mouth, and the door slammed shut behind her. She wore an old-fashioned pageboy, carefully smoothing down the gray with hairdressing, and harsh theatrical pancake makeup on her face with extra powder to absorb the desert sweat.

"Early?" I repeated. "I don't know." I looked around, and answered, "I don't think so."

"Darn tootin', you're early." She hoisted the tinfoil off the platter as if it were enormously heavy, and pushed the platter toward me with a little grunt. "Here, have some pork to while away the time." There was a pork-chop landscape as far as the eye could see. She puffed on the cigarette that hung from her mouth and bent over with the popping sounds of bubble wrap in her bones to pick up the kitten asleep in her lawn chair. It coughed little kitty-cat coughs and squinted at the smoke, but she said, "There, there, you're such a fussbudget," and held it close to her while it clawed at the skin tags on her neck to get away. She didn't even seem to notice.

I pulled the fork out of my jacket pocket and she said she had a fork for me, but I held up my hand and told her it was a special fork. With a knowing twinkle in her eye, she batted her special eyelashes made out of sable and said, "Tweety Bird, they're *all* special forks."

Trying to straighten out the thumbing hitchhiker tine on the edge of the counter, I pressed too hard and it looked like a woman's toes after being in heels all day. I spit on it, wiped it to a dull shine on my crusty pajama pants for good luck, and stabbed it into a burnt pork chop.

"Twenty-one fifty," she said.

" 'Twenty-one fifty' what?" I flinched my fork out of the pan and looked at her in amazement.

"Throw in another twenty if you want one of my photos, and another five if you want it signed. I'll have you know we're legitimate enough to take credit cards."

"Credit for pork? Huh? I don't even like meat all that much. Maybe I could, uh, get a smaller one then?"

"A smaller what, hon?"

"Pork chop. I didn't know your pork chops were so expensive."

"They're not. They're a buck fifty." She smiled and looked at me out of the corner of her eyes like a shadow of the flirty little girl she must've been at one time.

I tilted my head. "Huh? Surely—"

She cackled and smacked her knee like playing the spoons. "—and don't call me Shirley!" The bubble-wrap-popping sounds of her joints happened quickly as she gently doubled over to giggle and cough.

I smiled weakly because we were talking about my money and I didn't have twenty bucks to be dropping on pork, so I pressed on. "What's the extra twenty bucks for? Tax?"

She coughed, and in that instant, the struggling kitten ejaculated out of her embrace. She cleared the last of the rubble from her throat, popped her spine back up, and started to wipe down the counter even though nothing was there. "Aren't you here for the oncological hoedown tonight?"

"No. No, I don't think so," and I told her how I'd found the place. The part about bending a tine with my teeth, then throwing the fork up in the air.

"Oh yeah, sure, that's how most folks get here." She shook the crumbs from her rag over the ground and winked at me. As usual, I couldn't read the wink. I couldn't even tell whether she was sweet or mean. "We all find signs however and wherever we can to give us the shiny new hope we need," she told me while she folded up the rag and pushed it away from her.

"So how does everyone know to go up and flip a bent fork for where to go next?" This was just too incredible. There were very large forces at work here. Very large.

"You're too literal. You kids always are. I mean everyone gets here because their own signs tell them to take certain directions."

I wanted to tell her how old folks were always too general, when she said, "Here, taste," and handed me a slice of barbecued meat on a fork that looked just like the one that brought me here. "Well, that's because it is."

"It is what?" I nearly choked.

"It is from the same pile of forks that brought you here. Where do you think I get 'em? Why do you think I call this place Pork on a Fork?"

"I thought it was called Pork in the Road."

"Oh, yeah, that too. I always say that you shouldn't get too attached to one particular name. You've got a right to change your mind. Well, it's also called Pork on a Fork because I don't give out plates. You can't complain about the cost of paper plates when you've got an endless supply of forks. You've gotta work with what God gives you. I just do what God says. I figure it's your business where you put it once I give you the pork on the fork."

"Is it limitless?"

"Dunno. I only take what I need. You never take the babies, you know. It's the white man who'd come slaughter all the buffalo, take all the forks, salad, dinner, and dessert, and then one day come to find you've got no forks left, see?"

I halfheartedly nodded as I looked at the beautiful landscape around us and chewed.

"So aren't you kind of early yet, Tweety Bird?"

"What do you mean, 'early'? Early in a general sense?" I picked up another bite of pork and chewed. "Or a specific one?"

She peeled her thinning ostrich feather boa off like the paper on a crayon, and bundled it carefully onto a folding metal chair for later, revealing pale white skin, mottled with a few light veins. Faded blue ink on porcelain china. And she had the biggest breast I'd ever seen—talk about your checking sofa cushions for change. Don't waste your time when you've cups like that around. Or rather, she only has one full cup, and it runneth over—it's a sixty-five-pound breast.

In one smooth routine, she absently scratched at the flat side of her chest where her mastectomy scar must've been, unsnapped the top button of her tight black pants, and slowly sat in her lawn chair with all the popping sounds of her body. Parting her greasy lips and sighing all the way, she leaned her powdered face in the sun and said, "Whooee, I'm sure pooped. Well, let me be the first to welcome you to Area 54, Tweety Bird." She curled her lips under to make them small and she wore thick, unblotted lipstick so her cigarette would stick to her top lip when she talked.

She handed me some 25 SPF lotion and told me, "Be careful, because if you lie in the sun so much, you'll get skin cancer." But I tell her I lie in the sun so my teeth will look white and my bad electrolysis scars will fade. There's no sun like there is in the desert.

Things were different there, unlike the fluorescent lights of America, where everyone looks like they're lying, and I'm glad they've got it set up so that the Latte People won't all move in here. A place where the air is poison, the sun will kill you, and there's only iceberg lettuce with green goddess dressing.

She went on explaining that they were at ground zero, and poor people with cancer go out there because there's radiation. And as long as they're out there, they might as well have barbecue so she can go on stuffing five-dollar bills down her bra.

She really does have the biggest breast, but she didn't have the health insurance for it when things went wrong inside. She needed radiation so she moved out to New Mexico, where all the pigs were killed in the fifties. "Hon, can you feel the pig spirits?" She gazed all around in silence. "Pig vapors are everywhere. They are intelligent, and help heal us," she said and took a drag on her cigarette and exhaled. "Honest to God and the Lord Jesus Christ.

"Swine have always given so, so much"—she exhaled with a rumbling, throaty reverence as she looked at the platter of pork chops, and then squinted at the atomic test sites in the distance, gently scratching where her other breast used to be—"and ask for so little in return. Poor things. They were once warm with fur, but had the fur bred off of 'em so they'd be easier for eating.

"You know, their meat is the closest to human density . . . or so I've heard it said." She winked at me. "Yep. They have always been the *other* white meat, or as they say in Germany, *de anderen fleisch weiss*, and chicken is the norm by which everything else is judged. That just isn't right. There's so much more to life than comparing everything to chicken, see?

"Besides, chickens are nasty, dirty little birds, you know. Dirty, dirty." She shook her head in disapproval. "They don't have any lips, see, so they're always eating with their peckers. Just dirty as sin, I tell you. Honest to Pete." She smiled. "So whenever you're thinking that life is not fair, you think of the other white meat and that'll set you right as rain."

She continued to tell me how the fires never go out, and with all the plutonium that's still smoldering, you don't need briquettes. "Just pick it up with barbecue tongs and throw the meat on. So, Tweety Bird, what's your real name, anyway?"

I couldn't remember what I was calling myself these days— Joline, Tomato, or Mad Dog—and she didn't have the attention span for one of my answers, so she continued.

"—Well, then, Tweety Bird, as I was saying, this is the barbecue center of the world. Or at least, it should be.

Trucks stop here. That's why I call it a truck stop. Live briquettes, honey, go pick up some nickel that's on fire. Something that's seriously throwing off the isotopes, subatomic particles that keep hopping off atomic material."

They were curing themselves with nuclear decay. Eating pork cooked with isotopes. "People with cancer love it," she said. "They swear by it. It's got some healing properties."

She spit her cigarette off into some distant sand and patted the flat part of her chest. All around us were bright pink cigarette butts that were dangerous and pretty, and the sand looked like one of those ashtrays that used to stand next to an elevator.

"To some people it'd kill 'em," she continued. "We cater to all the people that can't afford none of those cheap-ass HMOs. Only thing is, it's all pig meat so the Muslims and Jews don't come out here as much. They don't eat pig meat, you know. And even though I love the Lord Jesus Christ, I was afraid it'd become some kind of Christian thing, so for the Muslims and Jews, I came up with cranberrium and rasberrium milk shakes—talk about flossing, this is the milk shake that flosses! Good night!" She clapped her leg and got lost in a fit of coughing and laughing and bone popping.

As we sat around, I found out that she's proud of smoking and drinks Tab with a little Jack Daniel's in it. "I like whiskey in my water and sugar in my tea." She sees fewer and fewer convenience stores carrying Tab and says she goes inside and says, "Don't worry. Stock up and I *swear to God* I'll buy what you got."

Her name's The Fabulous Tiki "Boom Boom" Ravelli: The Turkish Lassie with the Exciting Chassis/The Peeler/The Queen of the Educated Torso. She's a real old doll, and she jingles when she walks. She's lived through three husbands and wears tight pants. Her stomach sticks out a little.

I asked, "Are you really Turkish?" I was trying to whiten my teeth in the sun, stretching my body out like a short attention span in the chaise longue, and imagining my skin and insides sizzling like the atomic pigs of yore.

"Heck no, darlin'. That's just a bunch of piffle. But the strip joint had always wanted to use the tag line 'The Turkish Lassie with the Exciting Chassis' for one of their girls, and so I instantly got it when I came along because they thought I was so exotic with my last name and unbleached hair."

"Well, so what do you want me to call you?"

She shooed the question away and answered, "Oh, don't go to too much trouble, honey: 'Miss Fabulous' is mighty fine by me."

I tapped on my **breastbone** in simple introduction. "Tomato."

"Hmmm . . ." She shook her head, turned around in her chair and looked all around her, and sighed. "I'm afraid, Tweety Bird, that we don't have no tomatoes here. I've gotta admit that I'm a little ashamed 'cause even though I'm Italian, they give me agita. The barbecue sauce gives me heartburn as it is."

"No, that's my name."

"Well, yes, I suppose I could always buy you some tomatoes when I go back into town next week.

"Anyway, to answer your question, I got started when some boys in high school secretly watched me undress in the locker room. Word spread like the clap and from then on, when I walked through the halls they all called to me 'Ravelli, Ravelli, reveal yourself to me.' And I did.

"I gotta admit, I kind of took a shine to it, and when I found I could make a living as a tease queen, well, the rest is history. 'Boom Boom' was my first stage name. Yeah, then they changed it. Oh, I didn't get older—the clientele got younger—but they eventually changed my name to 'Tuesday' because it's not the best day of the week but it makes you *sound* prettier, and that's when I knew it was time to cash it all in.

"In my day, why, I was a real topper, I was. That was before they had to call me 'Tuesday.' I was so good as a table dancer, my heavens, I used to be able to scrape up gum off the sidewalk with my lower lips." She slowly nodded at the memories in her lap.

I was amazed. In the presence of a master. "Wow. That's something. I tried to pick up my motorcycle that way a couple of times."

"Hey, if Jack LaLanne can swim to Alcatraz with handcuffs on, pulling a tugboat in his teeth, well . . . let's just say, a little more practice, and you'll be able to pick up anything like the dickens. Good night!" She waved her hands and laugh-coughed. "Soon they said I couldn't even table dance anymore because of a couple of bad accidents where some clients got hurt, but like I told them, *Oh piffle!*—it wasn't my fault. What were they talking about? *I* didn't get bigger; the tables got smaller."

I nodded. She got even more of my attention with the mention of Jack LaLanne. In an economic era where there's something like six millionaires being made every day, and more Ferraris here than anywhere else, these little millionaire boys slouch in four-star restaurants and have tantrums for better service while drumming their silverware against the table to the hip-hop in their head. You can't tell me hip-hop hasn't already gone the way of "Disco Duck."

And through it all, Jack LaLanne's the only one to come the closest to actually being immortal without making some kind of fat-sucking, surgical Dorian Gray pact. Exercising in those jumpsuits, and telling us to get off our flabby little asses. When you hear little suburban millionaires talking about suck their dick this and that—oh man . . . it's time for Jack LaLanne and a great big coffee-table book about his endorphin smile to cover the rest of your *extra-fancy* New York books.

"But none of those names are my Christian name." She scratched her chest and continued. "No, ma'am. That's private, between me and God, and just for me to know, the way you've gotta have a secret zone all your own when you're rentin' yourself out by the hour. You know"—her arms and hands sort of flitted around her little frail body—"like your eyelids suddenly become erogenous zones."

For the first time, I was realizing how cool old folks can be and wondering why they're hidden away in drawers, out of the way.

But you'd never be able to stuff Miss Fabulous and her breast in any kind of drawer. She had only one old noble breast that could easily pin down a few boxes of crayons underneath, catch bad pig people in headlocks, and bring rulers of nations to their knees. But now it hung down low with exhaustion from being pushed into a thousand faces.

Like her quiet and tired breast, she just sat there in silence, chewing on a tattered toothpick, tracing the outline of her scar, thinking, until she jumped in her seat and said things were burning. And then she waved the barbecue tongs and finally said, "Stay! Stay with us here on our drag-queen planet. You can eat fresh fruit and listen to disco forever." And with a Fourth of July bubble-wrap finale, she popped herself up to the standing position and scampered away on the balls of her feet, and she was gone.

hen I woke up, she had thoughtfully draped a protective lead apron over my now barren reproductive organs as if it were an afghan, and the late afternoon sun was low in the sky, so it wasn't quite so hot. There were maybe twenty or thirty folks milling around the pool and sitting in chairs, gulping down armfuls of pork like Henry VIII, chain-smoking cigarettes, drinking whiskey and margaritas out of old, scratched-up 7-Eleven tumblers. The younger sixty-year-old ones had slathered themselves in sunscreen and the older folks were carrying umbrellas to shield themselves from the sun. You could tell who had sunscreen on because they kept on rubbing at their eyes. That stuff stings.

The Fabulous Tiki "Boom Boom" Ravelli was standing over me, and the first thing I noticed was how her other flat and empty bra cup was now quite successfully stuffed and coming to a lumpy point with five-, ten-, and twenty-dollar bills. The cup with the money stayed relatively light and close to her neck, while her real and tired breast hung low and kept to itself near her waist. The second thing I noticed was her handing me a margarita with one hand, and a pork chop impaled on a fork with the other.

I took the margarita in my right hand and offered up my lame left hand faceup like a plate. "Just drop it on my palm."

Miss Fabulous came around to the front of me. She'd changed out of pants and was wearing a wide, flowing golf-green muumuu appropriate for a desert evening of casual socializing. It had white prints of palm trees, and with her straggly red garland of a boa, made her look like a fresh young Christmas tree in a forest of bony cancer people. She pulled a lawn chair up and popped her bones as she inched her way down to it. Without saying a word, she started to feed me the pork on a fork.

Miss Fabulous twisted her head to the side as she tossed her red boa back around her neck, so the cigarette in her mouth wouldn't burn it. Then she tucked her flattened gray hair behind her ear, pressed it flat against her scalp. Popping her bones and leaning in so close they sounded like knuckles cracking, she held the pork inches from my lips and stared at me with all the seriousness reserved for advice or bad news. I looked closely at her beautiful sable eyelashes. They were so thick, it was like looking at eyes through pubic hair. She pulled her hanging breast up onto her thigh so it'd stop pulling on her back and said, "Now let's talk about you. You have no idea what you're gonna do next, do you?"

"No." I put the margarita down and groggily wiped the sleep from my eyes and the grease from the corner of my mouth. I told her how San Francisco was turning into a country club where they'd have to fly the plumbers in when the toilets backed up.

What seemed like hours later, she held her hand up for me to stop, clapped her hands together under her lips, and said excitedly, "Heavens to Betsy, now we've got to figure out what to do with you. We don't have much time. In fact, after that story, I only have the attention span for a one-card reading." And from beneath the folds of her flowing desert evening muumuu, she pulled a deck of tarot cards out from under her breast.

Shuffling, her hands make magic, fanning them out and cutting them as if she's baking something and alluding to her former glory days. She's shuffling, cutting each card in. Fanning, cutting, folding. She wanted me to achieve, receive, and believe all the inspiration from the one card in this one-card reading.

She coughed as she tried to whisper, "Now fan the cards yourself, little Tweety Bird, and snap them closed again until you come up with a question or thought about a problem in your life right now." As one would imagine with somone lucky enough to have created such a name, the Fabulous Tiki "Boom Boom" Ravelli was someone who was richly endowed with both magic and ordinariness. Equally ordinary and magical.

I took the cards in my hands and they were so big and cumbersome, I dropped them on the ground by accident because I couldn't hold them right. Miss Fabulous just shrugged and discreetly itched her scar underneath the stuffed bra cup with the inside of her wrist. I picked the cards up and tapped the edges back together.

Similar to Flower Frankenstein's deck, they were thick and homemade out of dog-eared chipboard, but these were lightly stained with little circles of grease and barbecue sauce. On one side of each card was the hand-drawn suit and symbol. On the other side of each card was an old, rubber-stamped art nouveau design of meat and a horizontal fork, and in between the two it read, "Pork on a Fork, best barbecue/Area 54 at Ground Zero."

"Okay, now pick a card, Tweety Bird."

"Pick a card? That's it? One card is really enough? When my grandmother in Puerto Rico used to read for the neighbor ladies, she'd lay them out in a whole involved design and—"

Impatient, she picked the card for me. When she flipped it on its back, she sucked in her breath and looked at my face, covering her mouth with all of her fingertips. Facing us was the intricate drawing of a muumuu, not unlike her own, except for the hovering pork chop emanating rays of light above it. Surrounding the drawing of the muumuu, in neatly arched hand-lettering, were the words, HOOCHIE MAMA: THE OTHER WHITE MEAT. Studying the card, she wrinkled up her brow like the many, many folds of the billowy muumuu in the illustration and shook her head. "Lordy oh my Jumpin' Jehoshaphat, I can't believe it. Why, you've picked yourself the High Priestess card. Good night!"

"Well, *I* didn't really pick it; you did. And what priestess?" I asked. "All I see is a muumuu. Not unlike your own, I might add," nodding to her own figure.

She shooed away my question, and glared at me mysteriously instead. "Uh-oh, I was wrong," she snapped.

"Very wrong. I'm afraid you can't stay here, eat fresh fruit and listen to disco forever."

I had no idea what it meant. "Why? That was sounding so good. I didn't pick that card, you did!"

"Hmmm . . ." She held her cigarette between her fingers and tapped at her teeth. "Looks here like you've got to put on a muumuu and get to work."

"Why do I have to *wear* a muumuu? I didn't even pick the card, and besides, isn't that a little too literal?"

"Too literal? You're too vague. You kids always are." The Fabulous Miss Tiki "Boom Boom" Ravelli ratcheted her once well-educated torso up out of the chair and turned to leave.

"Wait a minute. Last time you said we're too literal, and that we always are."

She shrugged. "Well you are, Tweety Bird. But you *must* go for literal whenever God deigns to give you literal messages. You have to wear a muumuu because what's next is not about your body anymore. It's about what's up here." She tapped on her skull. "That's where you gotta focus your strength now. Now, don't go lollygagging and fighting the word of His Lord Jesus Christ, or you're gonna get in trouble. You'll probably get taken out in a trucking accident, so they can choose somebody else, and you don't want that. Best not to fight these things, Tweety Bird."

"Don't fight it? Don't you find it just a little too coincidental that you're actually the one who picked the pork chop muumuu card, and *you* already wear muumuus?"

The Fabulous Miss Tiki wagged her finger at me and raised her eyebrows in reproach. "Now, Tweety Bird, don't be such a pill; I already told you that I'd pick you up some tomatoes when I go to the store next week." She was ignoring me in what I'd learn was her special little way of changing the subject, and she demurely burped into her fist. "Aw, cripes, the pork chops gave me heartburn again. It's a back handed kinda love, you know.

"Anyway, I'll be right back. Just stay right here. I'm gonna go light a candle and think about all this." She coughed a little stomach acid from her throat and produced another cigarette from under her breast, inside the muumuu, so I'd never have to wonder again where babies actually came from. "Hmmm . . ." She lit it, flicked her last dying one away, and tapped an arthritic finger to her greasy,

bubble-gum-pink lips. "I'll find you a muumuu while I'm inside. I think something brown to go with the brown of your eyes, and you'll be a topper, too." And she snapped a rubber band back around the cards and went away, skirting the pool.

Finally, the other people went away, too, and still, I just sat there, trying not to fight the inevitability of a brown muumuu.

"Eek, gads! I'm pooped." Almost two hours later, The Fabulous Miss Tiki "Boom Boom" Ravelli returned, gingerly taking tired steps around the pool with a large UPS-brown bundle of fabric under her arm, and in her hands, she held a bouquet of a few forks with pork chop flowers at the top. "Hon, you've gotta eat *all* of this," Hoochie Mama demanded. "You must make yourself a strong gal for what you are about to do, my little Porkchop."

I figured that I must become strong enough to put on that brown muumuu, so I shrank back from all the pork she was pushing into my face to remain weak. It wasn't until I

was about to fall over backward that I took the forks from her hand. This gave her the free hands to unfurl the billowy, cardboard muumuu like the parachute in gym class.

"Look"—she slowly and loudly squatted down into the chair, pulled a cigarette out from under her breast, and waved her finger at me—"don't be such a pill. God has told you what to do and I'm here to help."

"No, you picked the card and you're supposed to wear the brown muumuu. I'm telling you, you'll be the topper. You really will."

"Is that all you think this is about? Brown muumuus? Well, Porkchop—"

"Tweety Bird."

"Good night! Your name's Tweety Bird?"

"No, no, no, it's Tomato. But all along you've been calling me Tweety Bird."

"I have? I'm sorry. Well, anyway, Tinker Bell, things are different now. I've gotta call you Porkchop from here on out. You'd better get the shoe on the right foot and understand that the Baby Jesus knows a heck of a lot more than you or I, and it says right here you've got a lot of work ahead of you, and that's just too damn bad." Once again, she pulled the pile of cards from underneath her breast and held the Hoochie Mama muumuu drawing up in my face. "I'm here to teach you, little Porkchop."

"Why me? You're the one who picked the pork chop muumuu card. Have you considered that maybe *you're* the one with a lot of work to do?"

"Hard cheese, little bean. I meditated on *your* card for *you*, fair and square."

"Oh sure, what does *that* have to do with it? That's like blaming English people's bad teeth on the weather or tea."

Exasperated, she sat up in a flurry of spinal pops and turned around three times looking for a way out. With her hands covering her face, she mumbled through gritted teeth, "You really are the limit! Look, hon, why do you think I even came out here and started this cheap radiation hangout?" She gestured at the grounds all around her with a puckered face, like she'd tasted something awful. "I'll have you know that I myself picked this very same High

Priestess card decades ago. Why do you think I wear this green muumuu, anyway?

"Why do you think I've got an endless supply of forks to keep this operation going? Because when you're doing what you're supposed to, God just makes it so much easier." She pulled out a cigarette and just waved it around unlit. "Wait and you'll see." She put the cigarette back under her breast and stared at me.

The spontaneous flicker of understanding in my eyes betrayed me and she let out a phlegmy chuckle and coughed into her hand. "That's right. Now you're getting it, tootsie. I'm already in the middle of doin' my own Hoochie Mama thing. Now it's your turn."

I pouted at the yards and yards of brown. It may have made the UPS man Mister Happy Happy Pants, but for me it was an insult of color. "Why not black?"

She ignored me without mentioning store tomatoes, and instead plopped down and crossed her little arms over her breast and tried to rearrange herself comfortably and catch her breath through her wheezing nose. When she'd calmed, she opened her eyes and explained, "Like you, Porkchop girl." She pulled the same cigarette back out and tapped it to the pink lipstick on her bottom lip and squinted her eyes. "See," she started mysteriously, in a low, raspy voice. "I was a fussbudget, too, at first. I'm a fightin' gal. But you can't fight your calling or else it's bad. Very, very bad. And I'm not pulling your leg, neither." She wagged her finger before lighting the cigarette and inhaling deeply with her eyes closed.

"What happens?"

"Oh, just bad things."

149

"What kind of bad things, exactly?—Chain-letter horror where you end up in jail and get evicted from home?" I laughed.

She opened her eyes. "Honest to Pete, smarty-pants, this is nothing to make light of. No, ma'am. Bad things happen. Very bad things. And unfortunately they might happen to everybody else if you don't do what you're told. There"—she made a locking motion over her lips—"that's all I'll say on the subject, thank you very much. We'll have no evil here, young lady." And she crossed herself with her cigarette.

"You pulled the High Priestess card, and that's that. What the dickens are you waiting for? The Almighty Lord Jesus

Christ has spoken about the Great Mother Goddess. The muumuu is the universal sign of her regal robes, her regal housecoat. She is ageless, and she is every woman at every time, starting from Eve, to the virgin, a whore, someone's mother, and maybe your own grandmother. She is our inner thoughts, our subconscious thoughts, our reasons for the things we do.

"Got it?"

I didn't, but I still nodded so she'd just go on.

Miss Fabulous sat up straight, closed her eyes, massaged her temples, and spoke out in a monotone. "Hon, your job *will be* to go back to San Francisco and . . . and . . ." She cocked her head to the side as if listening for a phone to ring. "Now I've lost it. Hmmm . . . my memory's not like it used to be, so I don't remember what exactly you're supposed to do. But like you said, the city's changing, and you have to fight, get involved, save something, or someone—I'm not sure." She opened her eyes and sat back. "Sorry, hon. I was sure a second ago, but now I'm not sure what you're supposed to do. It just went away like that [snap]. Maybe the Lord'll make it clear once you get there and lead you where I can't. Yeah. Maybe that's what'll happen."

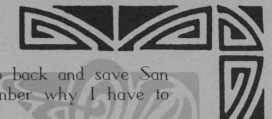

"Okay, fine, whatever you say. I'll go back and save San Francisco, but do you at least remember why I have to wear the stupid muumuu?"

The Fabulous Tiki "Boom Boom" Ravelli adjusted the lead apron she'd earlier laid on my lap and draped the muumuu proudly over my body. She pulled her head back to get a total view as if I were her daughter holding up a lovely wedding dress from Goodwill.

"The regal muumuu serves more than a matronly, high priestess purpose that matches your eyes: it'll serve as your cape of middle-aged-woman invisibility, and no one'll suspect you of wielding so much power, if any at all. As you wear it, you'll enter back across the Golden Gate into San Francisco like a Trojan horse.

"You'll be able to go anywhere: sneak pig heads from the butcher shop into real estate agents' beds; and when you're tired of doing whatever you're supposed to be doing back there and need a break, you can even slip into movies for free. No one will ever suspect you of a thing."

"Sneak pig heads into Realtors' beds? And your Lord Jesus Christ wants me to do all that?" I smirked, but if God had

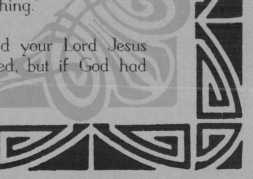

the vengeance of a Puerto Rican *mamacita* writing bad words in lipstick all over a cheating lover's car, then we're all gonna be saved.

Glaring at me with unbelievably wide eyes, she hissed, like a pig cat. "Now, I already done told you, I'll pick you up some tomatoes when I go to the supermarket next week. Let's hear no more of that. You really are a pill, good night!" She winked at me.

As the sun set in the atomic sky, she went on to teach me how to be invisible. She said they'll only notice you if you're skinny, pretty, and young. They're like a bunch of fucking predators. But if you don't want them to see you, you've got to be fat, old, and poor. "I know this because I was an old swindler and you've gotta use stereotypes to con people/they're not expecting anything else! Use that in your FAVOR!—Don't you see the beauty?"

"What does that mean?"

"I don't know how to explain it." She leaned in closer and shook her breast at me before continuing in slow, deliberate words, "But I know that you know. Every woman knows. There are dark secrets, ugly, evil dark secrets behind everything lovely. Balance. It is the only thing in life that is truly fair." And she nodded.

"Now look, my little pork cutlet, I know you're not crazy about the muumuu, but it's either that or you must get extremely fat, and the muumuu's easier to get in and out of. But they accomplish the same thing. You see, as people get older or fatter, I mean really fatter, not just so you look bad in your clothes, but *fat*, you are capable of disappearing. Why is that? It's because of magic. It's because people want you to disappear. If you go into a restaurant the same time as a skinny white girl, who's gonna get seated first? The skinny white girl. You might as well be off robbing a bank right then, because if you're not something to fuck or fear, then you're invisible.

"So you can string together all them little disappeared moments and become invisible whenever you want."

I wasn't totally understanding, but I listened.

"You see," Miss Fabulous explained, "when you're a stripper and taking off your clothes in public, you're multitasking. You're naked, holding in your stomach, you're smiling, and you're also working. You're making a paycheck. You still have to pick up the dollar bills in all of the five physically challenging ways, but it's also payday."

She went on to relate how she had these enormous breasts, and this was before implants. People couldn't take their eyes off her. She could stand in line at a bank and get paid for it because they stood straight out. During WWII, they looked like torpedoes, like every military wet dream you've ever seen. Gun turrets, torpedoes, everything.

"Twenty years," she continued. "A good twenty years of kitchy boom boom. And then I got The Sickness: breast cancer." One of them got cut off and was made into an expensive lotion in Japan so that certain people could catch money in the streets, enabling it to stick to their hands without slipping away. "I can't even afford the darn cream that was made out of my own breast." And her own moneymaker was not working anymore.

She still had kitchy, but she didn't have boom boom.

And she noticed that by kind of being such a freakazoid with one really huge breast, there were times when people just had to look away. She learned that people would avert their eyes and give her psychic distance. Some were scared and disgusted and had to look away. For twenty years, she felt people feeding off her and looking at her, and all of a sudden she realized she had the power to make people look away. Avert their eyes. Give her psychic space. Some did it out of fear of mortification of the flesh, while others were more gentle and just wanted to give her some psychic privacy.

"At first you lament the fact that you're not who you were." But she figured out how to string these moments together for her benefit, to become invisible and do what she had to do and get what she had to get and to pee where she had to pee.

"Reinvent yourself." She was wiping her hands on a huge motel towel. "We were all pretty once, but you're gonna have to grow yourself a pretty good personality before it's too late, anyway, so you might as well learn now. Some of the sad girls hold on to beauty by their nails and their youth by the skin of their teeth and watching some folks age, well, it's a whole lot painful. Like watching them scream and fall off the old cliff of Life in slow motion."

And we came up with a plan.

We're laughing, and laughing, and it's starting to make a lot of sense. She's becoming more real, like the Velveteen

Rabbit. And like Newton's apple falling on his head, there's not only a lightbulb above the head but the lightbulb filaments are going $E = mc^2$.

I realize that everything she's saying is at a level of poetic brilliance. I hear her as if everything she says comprises the laws of nature. Like I'm listening to the music of the spheres. Galileo, Newton. The reincarnation of everything that was ever said about fire, science, archaeology—all the "ologies" PLUS good pork anytime day or night. I was not just getting a warm shower, I was getting spiritually refreshed with life, liberty, and the pursuit of real estate values. Here was my chance to reinvent myself and become a better person that even Mr. Vegetarian Janitor would've been proud of, because with all the freedom I'd simply inherited, I carelessly spit it out like I was tasting wine. When would I swallow?

Now. I had to swallow the fear, the courage, along with the robustness of choice and sometimes dizzying consequences. Yeah, I used to have big plans as a big girl in little clothes; now I had big plans for a big girl in big clothes.

It all seemed like a brilliant idea—how everything was parallel, a coincidence, yeah: a sign. Right down to how we were both wearing muumuus, and how neither one of us used our Christian names, and The Fabulous Tiki Ravelli had the same basic initials as me, Tomato Rodriquez: "T.R." The same letters I had left when I covered up the "iumph" on my new yellowing bike with duct tape.

I wanted to be just like her. She had a charm bracelet with a little souvenir from every man she'd ever been with. Of men, she says: "Honey, they just get you dirty." As I looked at her squinting in the sun and rooting around for her green-tinted sunglasses, I knew that I was in the presence of skull staples and grounding reality.

And right then and there, as I accepted The Fabulous Miss Tiki "Boom Boom" Ravelli as my personal pork chop master in this Hoochie Mama Land, the muscle control came back to my floppy carpal tunnel hand like air being blown into a balloon. From there I learned the power of the educated torso underneath my muumuu of invisibility, and she taught me how to pick up my motorcycle with my labia, and finally she taught me how to use my fighting crayon for good. For the future. For the good of the future. For the future of good.

The cartoon suggestions from the superheroes of yore were finally having their Saturday morning way with me.

Saturday mornings used to be so full of hope, right down to the sugar at the bottom of the cereal bowl, and they would be again, even if it was like tucking my own stomach full of stretch marks under my plus-size muumuu dress and bullishly calling my UPS man "Daddy," because pretty is as pretty does.

God and the superheroes were calling. It was my turn, and now we're somewhere in the middle of my final story of how I saw my knuckle-cracking last chance to finally do good and to fight for something bigger than myself, out of respect for the people who'd fought tooth and nail for forty-hour work weeks, the right to vote, and the right to drink out of desegregated water fountains and paper bags.

The Fabulous Tiki "Boom Boom" Ravelli was echoing some of the same things that colored civil rights leaders like Malcom X and the Black Panthers had said about greed, beauty, self-esteem, and power. But what she said was finally specific to me in terms of being a woman. And although she spent her life serving pork in myriad ways, as the white woman, Miss Fabulous *was* also herself The Other White Meat . . . or as they now call her in Mexico, *La Otra Carne Blanca.*

I'd been given a vision, permission, power, magical power. I was given the directive to ride back into the city with my sword drawn, riding at a hundred miles an hour with boxes of crayons under my Kentucky Fried Chicken tits, wearing an invisible UPS-brown superhero muumuu to deliver the message of Hoochie Mama and save the last of the sex-havers and crayon people.

And who are the crayon people? The ones who make $6.50 an hour and have attitude problems, of course.

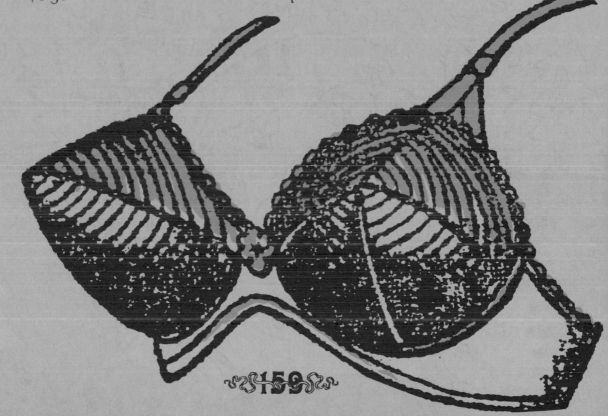

banana seat →

TRIXIE
↓

egg shell blue eye shadow

Tattoo of a rose →

Bikini Kat™ + Trixie travel through a melted-down ice cream sundae, called the DESSERT Desert. At the end of the day Bikini Kat calls out {smart} {stylish} {sassy}™ + Trixie's banana seat expands into a SUPER CAMPER DOME!

THE OTHER SET OF LIPS

round the crack of dawn, there was a detour sign up ahead and I slowed my way up to it and stopped. There was a problem with the bridge ahead, so I pulled out my map. I looked all around me and I was still deep in the desert. Tumbleweed was blowing, and in the distance was an old school bus about far enough away to be the size of a Tonka truck.

"Hi!" I waved to what appeared to be an old man and a young boy sitting in a couple of lawn chairs in front of their bus house with a lit tiki torch. They just drank from their mugs and looked at me.

I shrugged and looked over my map. The detour would take me way out of my way. I'd have to double back quite a distance to catch the main highway back to California and I didn't want to do that because I wouldn't get far by the middle of the day, and my muumuu would surely end up around my neck at seventy-five, eighty miles an hour.

I looked at the kid and the old man. The kid smiled and clapped his hands with splayed open fingers. I got the skunk eye from the old man as he scowled and shook his head.

Something about the knowing way in which he looked at me chilled my blood. It was as if he actually remembered something I'd done to him. But what? Fearfully, I slowly started to walk toward them so I could ask what.

And as if the little boy could read my thoughts, he jumped and hopped up the stairs into his bus house. I stood still. Seconds later he came out with a blue binder under his arm. I could make out the crudely markered lettering on the front. It said: *Bad People, Vol. IV.*

The little boy plopped back in his seat next to the old man, and flipped through what appeared to be a sheaf of laminated loose-leaf pages of bad people.

The kid held up his binder. I couldn't see that far away and so I tilted my head. That's when the boy ran up to an imaginary halfway point between us in the sand, dropped the open book, and sprinted back to the lawn chair, leaving a spray of sand covering the page of evil in this fourth volume of badness.

I carefully walked up to the binder of *Bad People, Vol. IV* and pushed the sand off the laminated pages. There was a grainy Associated Press photo of me, with bleached-blond hair, dragging a kid's wagon of guinea pigs to tout my ten-pounds-off prison diet after my release from prison.

Snapping the book shut and dropping it back to the ground, I held my hands up in the universal gesture of surrender. Then I smoothed my hands over my hips and legs, and tried to pull my muumuu taut so they'd see that I carried no weapons underneath the yards and yards of harmlessly cheerful brown fabric.

I hadn't had to deal with this since I first got out of jail. Instead of printing photos of lost children on milk cartons, the same advocacy group now wanted to print photos of anyone who got arrested on the back of potato chip bags, too. I was followed around convenience stores and supermarkets until the next batch of arrests came in and that seemingly endless shelf life of chips was bought out. We're in a society that's gone from watching out for lost children to looking for the bad people. Remember: gentrification isn't even about making things right; it's now about being safe. Very safe. No ripples.

I backed my way to my bike and discreetly mounted it. As usual, I turned it around with my feet, and as usual, I slipped on the dirt road and dropped the bike. Gasoline was gushing out, but this time I managed to jump out of the way while holding my muumuu over my chocha.

Before I'd left in the dark of that wee, early morning, I slipped on the UPS-brown muumuu that reflected the brown of my eyes, and looked at myself in her full-length mirror. I looked like a big brown talking mountain with a little head on a children's afternoon show.

Miss Fabulous came up behind me, smacked me on the rump, and lit her last cigarette in my presence. "Well, now, Tweety Bird! I see you're going commando. You sure you don't want some squirrel covers?"

I'd imagined that this old baby doll had ostrich feathers on her underwear, so I vigorously shook my head as I laced up my boots and answered in my scratchy little chicken morning voice, "Panties would only get in the way of everything we're trying to accomplish here."

And she knew I was right. When she hugged me with that big breast that held you at arm's length, she said, "Bye now. Say 'hi' to Broadway for me, and make sure you go and tell Alma Jean to talk badly about chickens."

She never did tell me who Alma Jean was, but no matter. I didn't think I'd ever feel so free, you know, being as asexual as possible by wearing a brown muumuu and straddling my new yellowing motorcycle without any panties on. If I wiped out, road rash alone would turn me into one giant scab, but no matter.

And this simple, little decision to entirely let go dictated a much slower, less populated route back to San Francisco because I didn't know how well the hem of my muumuu would stay tucked between my legs and not blow up around my neck.

But now, in the gray of the dawn, as I pinched the hem of the muumuu between my legs in front of a man and a boy who knew too much about me as it was, I was wondering if overall I'd made the right decision after all. How do we ever know? Any amount of change always sucks, first ride around the block. I guess we only know if we're doing the wrong thing if it still sucks a month later.

I grabbed the handlebars and started to heave it up. I saw the man and the boy hesitate and slowly get up from their seats but I violently waved them away; I wanted to do it myself.

And then I remembered the lessons of my master and I yelled for them to turn around. "That's right," I yelled. "Aaaall the way around!" When they blew out the tiki torch and turned their chairs around, I lifted the hem of my muumuu just above my knees, stood over my bike, and started to squat down.

This wouldn't work—not without The Fabulous Tiki "Boom Boom" Ravelli!

I kept squatting, feeling the strength of the muscles in my thighs as I slowly lowered myself close enough to feel the heat radiate off the chrome between my legs.

"Don't turn around yet! You don't want to get all embarrassed now, do you?" And they waited politely with their backs to me.

And there I was, just hovering above the warm metal of my bike, with my knees pressed close against my breasts, and I released the crumpled hem of the muumuu until it modestly splayed itself over my knees, past my bike, and settled in fluted edges around us on the sand. I was only a little head on top of a situation.

Can I do this? What the heck was I thinking?

In the wind, I felt a bony pat against my rump and it said, "*Come on, Porkchop, honey. You've no time to waste. Do like your Hoochie Mama showed you. Now come on, girl, you're fast runnin' outa gas . . .*"

I sucked in my breath and flexed my pee-holding muscles, not once, but seven, eight, and ninety times.

Breathe in . . .

Ready?

Yesss . . .

One . . . two . . . three . . .

[CLENCH]

With my newly educated torso, I pursed all of my orifices, and did it.

By the time I got the bike totally upright, there was a huge puddle of gasoline soaked into the dirt road./Enough to make mud, and that's a lot.

I wedged a rock under the kickstand, took off the tank bag, and unscrewed the gas cap; I had very little gas left. That meant I had little choice now; I had to continue with my shortcut over the bridge to make it to a gas station on a local road.

But what if the bridge really was dangerous? Question is, what was behind the barricade? Something scary? That's why a motorcycle is different. You can go places where other people can't. Motorcycles are special.

I looked at the kid and old man and their backs were still to me. "You can turn around now!" I called.

They moved their chairs back, and I looked down at the pile of gasoline mud, to the detour sign, and then back at them for a suggestion.

This time they both shrugged. The old man looked at the road ahead for a few seconds before he finally nodded. I pinched the hem of my muumuu close to me as I flung my leg over the bike, waved bye, and slowly pressed forward, expecting behind every cactus or rock to see monsters with peeled grapes for eyes pop out.

The sun was just beginning to come up and I came to a rickety wooden bridge over a deep, dried-up arroyo. It was only wide enough for one car at a time. At the edge, I saw a guy in a trench coat, straddling the fence on the side of the bridge, looking at the sunrise. When he turned to look at me, I saw a piece of paper flapping on his chest. I nodded hello and he wiped his eyes and I saw him start to shake with sobs.

I must've ridden ahead for ten minutes before it dawned on me that this guy might be trying to kill himself, and the new person I was being should make me turn around. So I turned around and pulled up near him and removed my helmet and lifted my goggles up to my forehead and asked, "Excuse me, sir, but . . . uh, are you trying to kill yourself?"

He clenched his teeth and shooed me away. "Go away, it's only a joke."

"A joke?" I slowly looked at the desert horizon all around me. Then I looked back at him and shrugged. "Which part is funny? I love a good laugh, some folks say I laugh at everything, but I don't—"

"—Please go now or you'll ruin everything."

"Oh, I get it." I nodded and laughed. "The joke hasn't started yet. Well, I always ruin anything, anyway. I tried to save a cat when I was a little kid once, but I scared it so much it darted onto a busy highway."

He started sobbing more, in a deep and quiet way.

I pulled out the ubiquitous dirty maternal hanky from the pocket of my muumuu, and it wasn't mine. "I know. The other side of comedy is pain. Depression is a real problem for you funny people. You know, the whole 'sad clown' thing." I walked closer to him and offered up my hanky. "I embroidered this myself," I lied for the second time in under a month. And in a small, ironic world, it was the tiny needlepoint of a sad clown.

"—No thanks, I have my own." He glanced at his watch. "Would you please leave?" he asked, exasperated. "I'm not trying to kill myself. I've got a plan."

"Is the joke on that suicide note pinned to your shirt?"

"Would you please leave?" He looked at his watch. "What time do you have?"

I smirked and sat on the ground to do some Jack LaLanne stretching exercises since I get so cramped on my bike that I hate because it hurt my hand. "You got an appointment or something?"

He rolled his eyes. "Look, just what time is it?" His voice started shaking again and he picked up some binoculars from his coat pocket and looked in the distance. "You're gonna ruin everything, you're gonna ruin everything," he almost-whispered.

I rested back on my hands and asked him his name.

"Fishstick."

I stared at the pink smears in the sky and nodded. "Yeah, I'd kill myself, too, if my name were Fishstick."

"Why do you say that?" he snapped at me.

"Oh, uh, nothing. Did your last, uhm, girlfriend give you that nickname?" I smiled apologetically.

"No, my mom did."

"Whoa. That's even worse. Straight from the mouth of the woman who changed your diapers."

"I'm not going to kill myself, it's only a damn joke. Don't you listen? Besides"—he looked at the rising sun—"what's wrong with my name?"

"Well, you'd only be named 'Fishstick' for one reason." I shrugged. "I mean, come on . . . if a girl's gotta guess, you're not gonna come up big. More like, 'Hey, is that a crayon in your pants, or are you just glad to see me?'—But I ask you, isn't it more about specificity instead of size? Isn't size more about casting a great big net out there in your pussy and hoping, praying that you reel an orgasm back in?"

Then he leaned against the side of the bridge and started crying. Like racking sobs crying.

"I forgot how you guys really are sensitive about this stuff. I'm sorry, so sorry." I got up and walked toward him with my arms outstretched.

"Get away from me!" He sniffled and lifted one leg over the side. "I'll jump! Get the hell away from me!"

There I was, chasing kitty cats into the road again.

"I was just here trying to get my girlfriend's attention. Ex-girlfriend," he corrected. And then he told me how she passed by there every day on her way to and from work, and he just wanted to talk to her one more time and she'd blocked his number and had a restraining order against him. She even wrote him letters about how she was meeting guys at the Cow Palace Family Steak House and having three-way sex with them.

I laughed because with all of the laws, demands, *and progress,* it was still so true: women will never be equal to men until they can walk down the street with a bald head and a beer gut and still think they are beautiful. All it takes is a third-base compliment to leave our panties bunched around our ankles and tits hoisted painfully over our bra cups.

"What are you laughing at?" he demanded.

"Oh, nothing." I looked at the ground and twisted my lips together like closing a plastic bag of bread. "First girlfriend, huh?" I changed the subject.

He nodded.

"Then unless she cheated, I suppose you're pretty clean."

"Huh?"

"Oh, nothing. Say, how did you get here, anyway?" I was puzzled that he hadn't seen the detour signs for this bridge.

He pointed below the bridge and there was a bike leaning against the red dirt wall of the arroyo, with bike tire tracks that came from the north end of the dried-up riverbed.

I nodded, and thought for a moment about having sex with a couple of guys in one of those shag, mudflap, squirrel pelt, mullet hairstyles who eat at any place called the Cow Palace Family Steak House. The iceberg lettuce salads alone in those little wooden bowls would have 45 grams of fat in places like that.

You'd not only have to make the first move, but all the moves in between, right down to the final one, where you say what great studs they are as you run your fingers through the short part of their Camaro cut, while smoothing the tangles out of the long parts in back.

I told Fishstick this. "Yeah, don't worry. That's no picnic, sucking off one pudgy suburban cowboy in front who's belching pork while sucking the marrow out of a chicken bone as another constipated guy's lazily bumping you from behind, trying to keep from peeing inside you."

I looked over and noticed Fishstick's face had that terror-stricken and disillusioned *What in God's name do you mean?* look that boys suddenly get when girls no longer seem plastic and accepting. I knew that look all too well, and over the years had learned to relish being able to please—then disgust—the opposite sex.

"Well, it's true," I continued to console him. "She can't be having *that* much fun with a couple of cowboys with hairplugs and saggy asses who go to the Cow Palace family eatery. You see, guys have one short midlife crisis—[snap]—it's over. But a woman can have the *Oh My God, Am I Still Sexually Appealing?* Crisis that can last from age twelve until she's forty-five—or until she's just too tired to act like the unpaid, unfulfilled porn star she's become, and enters middle age and menopause, when her pussy shuts down and she's free. Then she just stops giving a damn. It's a beautiful moment, let me tell you. I'm just getting glimpses—like subliminal film splices of a refreshing soda—and it's something else."

He still looked like he didn't understand.

"Look, throughout life, the reception of a girl's self-esteem crackles in and out with static, depending on how much she's riding her motorcycle or wondering if folks think she's lovable even if her tits sag—and sometimes, just when you think your esteem's in perfect tune forever, out it goes again. When you're young, the quickest, most soluble form of esteem is measured by how many people want to screw you.

"Some of us have got it all wrong: don't sleep with men on the first day you meet them. Men like to say 'hello' to a woman, and then go home and abuse themselves, fantasizing about doing it with her. If a woman deprives them of this opportunity, they get resentful.

"Now, here's where it gets tricky because 'resentful' has been mistaken as 'disrespect' for generations."

He sighed and asked, "You think so?" He seemed totally confused, but it wasn't important that he understand anything.

"But this is what your ex-girlfriend's probably going through if she's messing around with boys like those. I wouldn't be too envious, if I were you. To them, she's just another

experience to talk about around the lunch truck on Monday.

"And I'm sure your penis is just fine. Lots of women like ugly men with smaller penises because they make up for it with lots of enthusiasm and techniques and a fantastic sense of humor. Really."

I could barely hear him when he mumbled to himself, "I'm ugly?"

Fishstick was putting his other leg up over the edge and I ran for his back and ripped him off the bridge and to the ground flat on his back. "Stop it! Now just you cut this out! I'm really trying hard not to be selfish and to listen to you!"

"Ow! You're hurting me!" And I probably was because all of my weight was on my knee that was pressing into his groin as if it were a cigarette butt. If he wasn't small before, he was tiny now. Tiny like lipstick kisses and a small clown needlepoint.

"Okay, okay! I'm sorry." I moved it. "Hey, are you okay? Let's look. I want to see how little it is. I felt it. It was like the spine of a fish."

He covered his eyes. "Shut up."

"Come on. Let's see."

"It doesn't even matter anymore."

"Okay, fine. I've gotta go."

"It's about time. She should be here any minute on her way to work and you're gonna ruin everything."

"I told you, I always do."

"Well, thanks. See you around."

"Yeah."

I walked back to my bike and dumped some sand out of my helmet before I put it on. He went back to sitting on the edge of the little bridge.

"Okay, Mr. 'Ode to Billy Joe,' I'll be seeing you around."

He waved without turning around to face me. "Yeah."

I made myself laugh.

He didn't say anything.

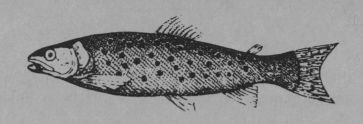

I waited for him to ask what was so funny. I removed my helmet. "Don't you wanna know what's so funny?" I finally asked.

"I said bye already," he said to the sky.

"Say your name real fast over and over, and it sounds like 'fish dick,' and it's kind of ironic being that you don't have a trout penis or anything, you know? I guess there are smaller fish like the ones they put on pizza, but by far the coolest fish is the Hicken Furbearing Trout. Now if you're looking for something funny, that's funny, and it's even true. It's got a full coat of fur below its fish neck.

"And speaking of mullets, there are mullet fish, and don't you think that the mullet fish would be the one with a full coat of fur below its fish neck?"

He flashed me a look that wondered if there wasn't a great, deep hole waiting for me somewhere.

179

"Okay, okay, I'm going, I'm going. Don't rush me. It's not like this is your personal bridge over troubled water or anything. If you were Canadian, you'd be a little funnier."

I revved the throttle more than I needed to. I just wanted to add to his little gothic prank as I took off. He mumbled something. "What did you say?" I asked.

He mumbled something again, but I ignored it. We were over. I was boring forward like an earwig. I had a destiny, a job to do.

As I was riding away, I wondered if he'd mumbled that he *was* Canadian . . .

. . . and considering my grubby sex history with middle-aged Canadian men away from home, looking for a good time, all that talk of bad Cow Palace mullet sex started me wondering if penises were so bad after all.

Turn-ons are complicated. Roses, chocolates, and shiny things are wonderful in real life. But fantasies of hopping naked and giggling around the corral while some rhinestone cowboy chases you around on an uncooperative big blue ox so he can hog-tie you in order to make all sorts of demands you could never, ever possibly meet—well, let's just say there are no words to convey the power of this kind of fantasy. And if we were playing scissors, paper, rock, let's just say that they all would win, and they'd get the banner, the roses and chocolates and shiny things, anyway, as they sashayed down the runway.

I used to sashay down the runway in the auditorium at the YWCA's modeling and charm class when I was a little kid. That was after I pretended I was the Fonz in third grade and threatened to beat up two girls named "Sally." I never did. They had big boxes of crayons with the extra-fancy sharpeners in back. I always ended up sitting next to them in the Brownies with my really long pants rolled up around my ankles, making fruit faces with half a canned pear, raisins for the eyes, and a maraschino cherry for the mouth. I thought the Brownies and fruit faces was stupid; not nearly as amazing as the three-dimensional snail wall hangings my mom made on colored burlap hanging from dowels.

I only wanted to beat up the Sallys because their moms volunteered for so much, the teaching staff just sat in the back of the class smoking cigarettes. That's where I sat laughing with the only big, hyper Korean kid in all of West Virginia. Kenneth.

Truth is, sometimes even I want to be small and tiny. I want to be the kind of little girl in a wisp of a dress that a man has to warm up under his armpit before he mounts her. I want to be little more than a hand-knit penis warmer with a couple of flailing arms and legs sticking out on either side like a faucet knob. They like that because it makes their penis look like the Empire State Building.

I just want to curl up on their laps and ask them all about the big, wide world. I want to suck my thumb, their thumb; I want to nuzzle up in their Santa Claus beard and smell free things for Christmas.

I want to wear *Hustler* beaver-pink gowns and jewels for them, paint my nails and twirl around atop their rock-hard refrigerator penises like a wing-nut or a jewelry box ballerina. I want them to call me their "little girl" and I want them to lead me around the corral on Paul Bunyan's big blue ox without any panties on. Then, as I'm delicate and tire easily, I will nap in a little matchbox without drooling.

But we're supposed to choose one size, one sex, one look, one rigid role like a high school persona. Nancy boys and girls who felt different ran away to San Francisco to be near other nancy people, with the tacit agreement that we'd dress and think alike so we could recognize each other and stick together. This eventually becomes just as rigid as the heterosexual culture.

At the height of the lesbian fad, movie stars scratched and kicked their way in front of the cameras, promising their public that if they weren't lesbians now, they'd watch porn movies and become so later. And now that famous lesbians were shackin' up with the teeny, little movie stars/and now that gay boys were having children/and now that lesbians were out in the suburbs mowing lawns/and now that all the butches had gone from merely wearing jackets with men's names on them to cutting off their tits, and *becoming* men—lesbianism had become something else entirely.

The only way left to rebel was by having illicit heterosexual sex with a big hairy man who lets you call him "Dottie."

You may think I'm kidding about some of the dissension among the Rainbow ranks, but before we stopped talking, HONDO Flammers used to tell me that after sucking each other off in the saunas, the gay men would pad behind him into the locker room, nervously gather around him, giggling like twelve-year-old boys, and ask him questions about

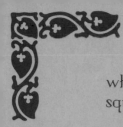

what it was like eating pussy: "What's it like, huh? Is it squishy and gross?"

"Good God, man! We *rim* each other! How could that possibly be any *less* gross?"

And then they realized he could have a point there. Some would ponder his wisdom, while some would get inspired to start licking each other's asses. What men can do to each other in the privacy of those locker rooms with long wooden benches is mind-boggling.

And as our ranks thinned in San Francisco, it was apparent that we'd be forced to become more flexible and resourceful. I learned that in jail, your standards of pretty totally change; and you'd sell your mama down the river for a cigarette butt.

Already, with all of the gentrification and evictions, most of the underpaid lesbians couldn't afford to stick around, so the handful that was still here had to start recycling ex-girlfriends four and five times: "Okay, this time wear the red wig so I don't recognize you."

I called myself bisexual—even though I didn't think I'd ever have sex with a guy again—for the same reason I reserved

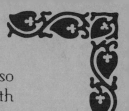

the right to be white once in a while and be stoic. And so I was surprised at my "resourceful" fascination with Fishstick. It didn't seem like his little suicidal penis would be so bad. And if it was small—for he didn't protest, or whip it out like a salmon the way a big dude would—then he wouldn't be so threatening. It would be like a small little white rabbit penis. Little pink eyes. Twitching nose and whiskers. Almost want to put a ribbon on it because without the fur it'd be cold and need something to wear besides Chanel No. 5.

Even though he was the kind of guy women didn't really want, and even though he was probably the kind of person who was into bad Internet humor, I now found him vaguely fascinating at this profoundly depressing time in his life. There was something thrilling about a guy who's willing to die, whether it's climbing up Everest to meet death and lose a nose to frostbite, or jumping off a bridge. Add to that the helplessly sexy element of an extremely depressed man who could be dead and stiff at any moment, and whoa—he brought out the best of my new carnivorously maternal instincts, and besides, a Canadian boy is perfect when you want to relive the *What's That?* moment you just kicked in the groin when you were young.

But weren't these thoughts bad? Cheap? I didn't care.

Besides, I wanted to relive the fresh and dewy *What's That?* moments I'd lost, even if they were through someone else's scared penis rabbit eyes. I suppose this is what the child molesters always admit when confronted at a cocktail party.

Because you see, for me, as the years tap-danced by after that childlike stint of writing in the closet, my evil crayon ways took a wrong turn. Turned away from Good and rode a banana peel into hell around the time I began to sleep with roll-on deodorant bottles wedged up between my legs to stretch myself out. I didn't want my first man to *know* he was my first one.

Because when they know you're a virgin, they start tickling you under the chin like a kitten and that wreaks havoc on your whole prepubescent bitch/whore routine. I was running with a rough, half-lidded crowd. The kind of people who had never been virgins, who had been born fucked and walked around with batteries balanced on their shoulders and dared their own grandmothers to knock them off.

Not allowing myself to have a benign crayon era with my virginity led me to a life of ordering Columbia House records under former neighbors' names, and I'd tell the mailman that, sure, I'd make sure they got it. And slippery as snot on a doorknob, that then led right into forging roommates' checks, kidnapping a cheating lover, running over a cat, throwing two-by-fours at yapping Chihuahuas, sleeping with married Canadian men who thought they were telling me things I'd never heard before. And I was a pretty good person, too. I never caused baboons to go berserk, and I never had those screaming fits whenever I was forced to go to a Quaker meeting. I'd even buy napoleons for the cranky old lady across the street.

But the truth was, everyone in San Francisco was buying napoleons for old folks, or taking casseroles to the terminally ill, and on the way out the door making sure the pencil jar's stocked with good pens in case they're inspired to change their wills.

The main point here is, once you start coloring wildly outside the lines and go out of your way to ruin your own childhood, then fling your maidenhood all around the high school cafeteria like a fatty piece of chicken skin, you're a drinking game away from biting caps off of beer bottles with your labia and shaving your skanky legs with the shards of the glass afterward. You miss all the innocently undressed *What's That?* moments in between where you see if twisting a penis into a poodle hurts at all. Or why testicles look so much like breasts and you stop the urge to call them breasticles because it's not as sexy as you'd think.

Sure, you can get those moments back again, but usually as part of that middle-aged grown-up game, where you're wearing those frilly ankle socks and size 18 baby-doll dresses, trying to hide that small pile of stretch marks on your stomach and licking the backs of your UPS driver's knees. It's just never the same as it was the first time around because you didn't have to roll your labia up like raw bacon back then. And plus, I was still ending up in some weird, embarrassing relationships I should've gotten out of my system way, way back in junior high.

But now that I was firmly nailed into my thirties, it was time to stop being so casual with what little sprints of energy I had left. I felt as if I were mellowing out a little, and it was time to use my carefree evil attitude for good. Maybe The Fabulous Miss Tiki "Boom Boom" Ravelli was right: maybe you do have to sometimes ask: what would Jesus do?

And if you don't agree with what he would've done because it's too much work, it's time to start doing a little soft-shoe moralizing so that you at least have a brief chance of getting ahead without the martyr option. I didn't know enough about the Hoochie Mama, The Other White Meat high priestess to know what she would've done.

And so as usual I wound up wondering: what would Andy Warhol do?—Or what would someone who even *knew* Andy Warhol do?

So I turned around and drove back the ten miles I'd gone. I saw the detour sign from this other direction and momentarily thought of following the rules, but I laughed at myself and drove on past.

I pulled up to him, still looking at his watch, lifted off my helmet, and asked, "Did you say that you're Canadian?" For an American woman who's never had health insurance, charging a socialist with access to national health care had its own added erotic taboo charge that antiquated dirty talk misses altogether.

"No, I'm Texan."

189

I waived the detail aside like a mosquito. "Same thing, you all just go around saying 'darlin'.' No matter, I'll still give you a blow job, for blow jobs fix everything." I smoothed his hair from his forehead and patted his cheek before I started marching back and forth in front of him. "There's nothing that can't be fixed by smokin' pipe. Look at Clinton. And if the Israelis and Palestinians would've sucked each other's dicks there'd be peace. Lots of peace. Peace to spare. We Are the World, Hold My Hand? No, baby: We Are the World, Suck My Dick."

I couldn't read his dry Texan squint, I couldn't even read animal tracks in the sand, but I could read the teepee in his pants. Running my finger over the bottom of my lip, I squinted back at him while I nervously cleared my not-so-deep throat. "But it's gonna cost you." I stepped back and spit a little subliminal spray in the sand. "Cost you big."

He scoffed. "I don't need to pay for that sort of thing." Turning away from the influence of the big, soft, warm hole in my face, he shook his head and said to himself as well as to me, "That's bad, very bad."

"Look, you'd be experiencing the kind of techniques that'd make San Francisco fags give me a tear-stained standing ovation."

Turning back toward me, he mumbled the inevitable, "Uh . . . well, okay, how much would I have to give you, to you know . . . that thing you just said?"

"You have to say it."

"I don't want to."

"That's why you must. This is all about stretching. Doing things we're not used to."

"I'm not that kind of guy."

"Oh, I can see it in the blood vessels of your eyes that, like any man, you're one uncivilized second away from *a patch of skin, a hunk of hair, and a bad smell: let's party.'*"

"You are evil like Eve."

"Yeah, sure. I am the secondhand-clothing lessons of Eve and handing you the pork chop in the garden of evil. Really, I am about as evil as a headache."

"Huh?"

"Never mind. Just *say* it. Say what you want." I insisted, because vampires can only come inside your house if you invite them in.

"Okay, okay." He looked at the ground and pushed sand back and forth with his foot like a windshield wiper. "How much do I have to give you to, uh, do that thing with your mouth."

"I guess that's close enough. Well, funny you should ask, little Fishstick." I clapped my hands, smiling as I skipped back toward him. "But the question isn't 'how much,' but 'what.' "

He looked up in surprise that set into suspicion. "Huh? . . . Well, then what do I have to give you?"

"There you go. Well, I need your pants."

"My pants?"

"Yes. I don't have any on under this, and you'll look even more pathetic to your girlfriend, anyway, if you're jumping off this bridge dressed like a flasher." It was a matter of

public safety because I now felt that the raw, unpanted power of my labia majora was too dangerous for the mere mortals out there in the world.

"Oh, of course. Fine, sure." He seemed confused, but unzipped his pants and rolled them down to his ankles and stepped out of them. He neatly folded them up into a square and handed them to me.

Before I saved his life, I removed his black trench coat, while he stood there in his stunned freshness, and I carefully placed it on the concrete ground in front of him for knee padding. Like a master sitting before a different piano, I cracked my knuckles and looked him up and down. "You must take off your shirt," I demanded. I explained how creepy and wrong men looked with just a shirt on and nothing else on bottom.

As he lifted his arms and peeled off his shirt, his armpit hair took me back to memories of an East Coast summertime. The landscape of his beige armpit was like the beach, and the straight armpit hair was the dried and frizzy grasses on the sand dunes blowing in the wind.

Dropping to my knees, I glanced behind me. There were no grasses or water in this parched and sandy desert, only tumbleweed and sagebrush blowing by like giant dust bunnies. The horizon poked the rest of the sun up out of curiosity, and my little fish boy nervously looked up and down the road.

I turned and looked at the road behind me. "Oh yeah, by the way, no one'll be coming across this bridge." I turned back to him. "There are detour signs on either side, to take the main road because if you wait long enough, this rickety old bridge will jump for you."

I felt his faint disappointment, but it quickly blew away as I flipped the elastic of his boxer shorts down over his fishy-looking penis and past his thighs.

He covered himself with both hands. "Please, uh, please don't make fun of my penis, okay?"

"Only the truly evil make fun of another's genitals, my friend." This is true./He had wee fins on either side. First, I greeted his penis in my traditional manner: I tried to stare it down as if it were a wild spider monkey caught unaware./Then I slipped the tip of his surprise into my mouth, licked the underside of humor, lightly grazed my teeth across dangling irony before taking suicide fully into my mouth and bending my uvula back as simply as the cardboard flap on a pack of marked cards, because this was easy as pie.

Sometimes it's the tickle of a stranger's pubic hair fluttering against your upper lip that finally gives you the inspiration to do something far more ambitious with your life, and so when he thrust his hips against my lips, I thought, "Rising property values!"

And when he tried to cram his little penis past my front teeth again, I thought, "Low crime rate!"

And when he pushed himself up to the edge of my uvula, I thought, "Good schools!"

For it was in that uvula-bending moment where I tried not to gag that I thought, "Eureka!" And now I knew exactly how to save San Francisco.

As Fishstick misunderstood my enthusiasm, he walked into my face and meowed like a cat stalking a bird out the window and I wondered: was now the time to swallow the fear, the courage, along with the robustness of choice and sometimes dizzying consequences?

No, with a penis in one cheek and a tongue in the other, now was definitely not the time. I pushed him back so hard he almost fell off the bridge.

Hicken's Fur-Bearing Trout

Rare, almost extinct, this fish lives in some arctic lakes and eats mostly ice worms

Billy Joe Fishstick had never been so sexually happy as when I went down on him on his bridge over troubled water. His eyes were still bulging. "Your mouth: it's just this, this, wonderful space in your face." He shivered, looked down at his still erect penis, and asked, "So, can't we please finish?"

I could've, but I didn't want to. It was no big deal to me. Giving head was like turning on a light. That's what I love about men. Coin tricks for five-year-olds are harder. But we had a lot of work ahead of us, so I said no.

I was pinching the hem of my muumuu between my knees with one hand and spraying oil on my bike chain with the other. "You know, the other Billy Joe jumped off the Tallahatchie Bridge because of an excellent blow job. But they can also be used to save lives."

I should've let him die.

"What's wrong?" he held out his arms and asked.

"Oh, it's not you. It's me," I said out of historic heterosexual habit, where you wrap your lover's ego carefully in newspaper and place it in a box with all of the other white lies. Truth was, with so much to do, I liked it better when he was depressed and quiet.

I forgot how boring and empty straight boys can be when they talk. Like a box of hair, they've got nothing much to say, and can't even help it, although some may try to like folk music and fight for causes and chain themselves to Green Party politics, but they're fighting against some pretty strong, uninteresting forces. It's hard to be full of testosterone and remain politically correct. Their women have to create a lot of drama out of jealousy and breakups, and channel their own histrionic emotions through them just to make men seem more interesting and bearable. That's okay because even interesting and bearable can get annoying.

As I listened to Fishstick chatter on, it was like being held under water. I thought I would run out of air and suffocate. Unfortunately *this* is how I end up feeling about all the chatty people I've ever seen naked.

I placed the cap back on the chain oil, wiped my hands on my muumuu, and went to the edge of the bridge to spit and admit to myself that most of the time sex was a waste of time and bad sex wasn't even worth showing up for. Big deal. The muumuu truth of it all that I could no longer hide from was the fact that I don't think I actually liked sex as much as I liked being around the other people who were having it.

Gay, bisexual, straight? I must be nothing. Asexual. I may be talented with boys because they're the ones I cut my teeth on. And girls can give the kind of pleasure that makes you call out for Jesus and lean against the edge of the bathroom sink and cry, but when it comes to lovin' women back in that porn-movie way that dares not speak its name, I'll always have floppy UPS driver hands, and I'll never be in charge the way I'd been with men.

But off-the-rack heterosexuality is so boring. The idea of it. The reality of it. The lifestyle of it. The rules of it. The hygiene of it. All along, I'd simply want to be treated with the same breathless reverence and fascination due any lesbian.

All that didn't matter now. Things were different, as muumuus have their own monologue and dialect. They never cry for REVENGE! shriek for JUSTICE! or caterwaul for your scalp. They're too tired. Instead, they speak in artery-clogging sighs, and ask, "Before you sit down, can ya just get me a Coke?" Or tell you, "I could use just a *little* more gravy on my mashed potatoes." The muumuu spoke the truth and reflected the way I really felt inside: brown and gauzy with lots of concealing fabric.

I've been straight, gay, colored, white, small, whatever. And now I was fat, invisible, and also I was old. I was no longer a child with clean little hands, tiny new teeth, apple juice breath, brand-new skin. With my new muumuu mind-set, I had to face the truth that I didn't want any more to do with the whole sticky humping/friction business. After wearing the magic muumuu, the cloak of invisibility, I understood the beauty of finally not giving a damn. Although later I'd learn that when I took it off, I'd suddenly *stop* understanding. Snap. Just like understanding directions from the gas station attendant until you drive away and it all becomes absolute gibberish.

"Give me something!" I demanded suddenly as I whirled around to face him.

"I don't have anything more." He smiled and held up his hands. "You already have my pants and everything in them."

As I was turning into every woman at every time of her life, I started to physically experience the part of turning into a straight girl who needed more. My insides spasmed, pulled, pushed, and I twisted around and dropped on the ground, feeling the need to pee, bleed, vomit up all the ancient ice cream binges of every woman in the world, and ask for pretty shiny things at the same time. I clutched a fistful of muumuu between my breasts and gasped for air. "It's not enough. You have to give me more. I need a souvenir, damnit, or I'll . . . I'll . . . I'll *die.*" I rolled my lips back, bared my teeth, and glared at him. "Hear me, man? I said I'd *die!*"

He just looked at me, but I couldn't have changed my mind even if I wanted to. He checked all of his trench coat pockets, but came up with nothing. And then he stopped, ripped the suicide note from his shirt on the ground, looked at it hesitantly, unfolded it and read. He laughed at what it said, looked back at my need, folded it back up and thrust it into my gasping fists.

Almost instantly, I calmed down, folded it up into a small one-inch square without reading it, got up, and walked over to put it into my new pants' pocket.

"Sorry," I said as I demurely covered my mouth as if I'd belched at a nice restaurant.

"I don't know." He seemed skeptical and worried. "Something really happened to you. It's like, it's like . . . well, it's like you turned into a thirteen-year-old girl at the mall."

I shrugged and ignored him. "Why don't you put your trench coat on. You can't ride with me in your boxer shorts."

"With you?" He shrank away.

"Sure. Don't be such a fussbudget." I walked toward my bike to leave. "What choice do you have? To wing back to your skanky meat-loving woman and hope it'll be the way it was before? Or be my sidekick?"

"Hey, what's your name, anyway?" he called out and shuffled a little closer. [SNAP] *He was mine.*

But now I didn't even know who I was anymore. Was I Joline, the daughter of my mother? . . . Or was I Tomato, the leader and sole member of the motorcycle gang Flaming Iguanas? . . . Maybe I was Mad Dog, the vengeful, half-assed lesbian who sucked in bed . . . Perhaps I should remain Tweety Bird, some old woman's generic nickname for a pipsqueak like myself . . . But maybe I *really* was

Porkchop, the faithful student of a Hoochie Mama high priestess? . . . Or had I gone beyond even that now? . . .

My second set of lips started to flutter and mumble something in reply, so I put my hands on my thighs and bent over as if I were trying to keep from fainting. But I was really listening. Listening to the whispers coming from between my legs. As I pushed my head in between my knees, I could hear what my vagina was telling me.

When I looked up, Fishstick was no longer in front of me, but behind me, looking at my muumuu-covered ass and jerking off.

I rolled my eyes in disgust. "Put that thing away."

"Wait, can you bend way over like that again? That dress is pretty hot." His voice was a-shaking and his hand was a blur. "Ask me if I had a good day at school, will ya?" His head fell back and he moaned.

"You're sick." I pushed his coat at him and he fell backward.

"You are evil," he moaned loudly.

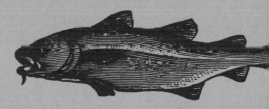

"What did you say?" I turned to him with a look that reminded him how I hadn't even made fun of **his genitals** quietly in my mind, but **he was** pushing it now that he was mooing like a cow.

"Nothing." Fishstick cleared his throat, got up and dusted his backside off. "You just never answered me when I asked your name and I was just wondering, well . . . I was wondering why. Like maybe your name is Mrs. Satan."

I pulled a stick of gum out from under my breast, unwrapped it—offered him one/the wrapper was translucent from the sugar melting in the desert heat—after I had bundled the muumuu under my armpit, slipped on his pants to cover my powerful and **OMNISCIENT LABIA** from the world, and zipped them up. After I absently itched my left breast and looked around to ensure privacy before whispering loudly in a voice tailor-made for a perfume commercial, I casually told him, "Yeah, well, my name is Mrs. Rodriguez. But just call me Hoochie Mama," and then after that, I tapped my lips with a couple of fingers in the place where a cigarette should've been just to try it on for size. But these were new days. We now knew better than to actually put one between our fingers in an era where we've got women polar bears in the arctic circle growing penises from PCB contamination.

And it felt all right. :·

POTTED HAM

When I was done with Mister Ode to Billy Joe on the bridge over troubled water, it was already late morning. So our morning after is the after. There's got to be a morning after, and ours was in the afternoon. And that afternoon I cleared my gear off the bitch pad on the back of my bike and made him sit quietly behind me with a little fishstick hard-on poking me in the back like morning. I was nice. I let him keep his hands toasty under the fold of my breasts because without a bra, I also needed the support. And as my trusty new superhero sidekick, I'd need him to give me all the support I could get as I tried to go back and save an entire city.

That was the last time I needed a man so much. After Fishstick, I'd decide to keep men in my life by naming tampons after them. A super-plus favorite of mine, named Fred, would wiggle his mousy tampon string, trying for a salute, and say "Hazzah!" because he never was much for creating his own imaginary world. Fred had to piggyback on others' already scripted out Renaissance fairs, Dungeons and Dragon role-playing games where they argue about what the elves would really do, and all of the generational Star Trek details. Oh that Fred. They're so real to me. So very real.

And after a few hours, I'd say, "Good night, Fred!" and hurl his bloody carcass away in a beautiful swan dive toward the toilet.

But for now I needed Fishstick intact, motivated, and as hard as my aunt Pad's arteries. I had the crayons under my tits, the invisible superhero muumuu, while riding a hundred miles an hour with my sword drawn. Everything was coming together like a wet kiss at the end of a warm fist, or whatever Bark used to say, for Fishstick was my sword.

Picture complete.

THE ROOT WORD FOR COLONIZE IS COLON

I started the engine like a chainsaw, unrolled the seat belt, quickly pulled it over my hips, and "click-clicked" it closed underneath the pile of muumuu fabric. Clenching the chain steering wheel with both fists until my sweaty knuckles were white, I concentrated as I revved up the engine of the rusty 1964 Cadillac Coupe de Ville. We'd just bought it from a recently evicted twenty-year-old Mexican grandmother with a lip-liner/chocolate-milk moustache, and a long, brassy ponytail pulled so tight, when she blinked her hairs plucked loudly from her skull like guitar strings.

She had seven classic cars, but only four small grandchildren and one little great-grandmother to drive them all over the bridge. Her daughter was in Canada finishing grade school so she could get Aileen Wuornos off death row one day.

That left one car she couldn't drive./So she sucked out most of the gas and sold us the Cadillac real cheap.

1964 was the last year they had fins. Wee fins. They reminded me of someone's penis. "You must feel right at home in this car." I smiled at Fishstick.

"Well then you must feel right at home in the backseat," He poked me in between my breasts.

I smiled and nodded my head. "Oooh, that's good." I lifted my finger in the air. "One point for the Fish."

He was actually right, but not in the way he thought. I'd never had sex in the *back*seat of a car, but I had learned the ruthless art of war there. The backseat acreage of a 1964 Coupe de Ville wasn't so different from the '72 Chevy Impala my mom used to drive my sister and me across country in when we were little. We'd punch out our baby teeth, claw at each other's eyes, and fight bloody, amputating battles over the free zone, which was about an entire foot of vinyl seat divider.

But now the stakes were higher./Much higher. We were fighting for the ultimate vinyl seat divider. We were fighting for the citaaaay, yeah. We were fighting THE MAN. Can you feel the funk? Can you taste the lucky penny trickle of blood in your nose? Feel the trickle of uncertainty in the crust of your eyes? Hear the clap of the ocean waves in your teeth? See the rush of promise in your pussy? Taste the crack of the country club pecans in your cleavage? And the smell of coffee beans in the condensation of your armpit hairs? It's all there, man, it's all there.

The idling engine roar sounded like the universe running down the street and ripping in half, and when I tossed it into gear, the wheels spun and squealed like running over a road paved with Chihuahuas. A road we'd all like to see. The car flew around the corner and leaped over the hills and the car came crashing down, with the crashing of steel, in an homage to Steve McQueen, leaving behind the gaping jaws of a kid delivering newspapers and a standing ovation from the kids at the lemonade stand and they are mesmerized by it for it falls just under on the list, after getting a blow job.

When the dog bites, when the bee stings, when he's feeling sad, the list of a man's favorite things is "Blow job, #1"/"Car Chase Scene, #2." Sometimes they're interchangeable. Most men say their ultimate fantasy would be watching two women; but they're just trying to impress each other. The truth is that they'd rather get sucked off while watching *Bullitt* or *The French Connection*. Which is the number two car chase scene? Always a major debate.

My funky emotions pulled out the pop gun and I blasted the radio. If listening to the Beatles made you worship the devil, Pink Floyd made you kill yourself, and if forcing fetuses to listen to Mozart turned them into boneless

suburban geniuses, then listening to the raw funk of George Clinton made you resist **THE MAN, FIGHT THE POWER**—all that and then some.

My mom's still not talking to me because of it. Can I help it that she, her big girlfriend, and my grandmother decided to go on a vacation in San Francisco in the middle of a revolution I was trying to lead? I wonder if Che Guevara ever had to sit with his family through a bourgeois evening of small talk at the Castle of Prime Rib?

Sitting there among the trappings of fine china and people feasting on coffee-table-sized cross-sections of cow surrounded in *au jus*—Oh, how they ate. I looked at the cow plasma streaming off every table like a tablecloth and self-righteously excused myself from my family forever. If it weren't for having to ask them for bus fare home, I would've stormed out of there a lot sooner, I tell you.

And now my mother's not accepting my collect calls, but a lot of it may be due to her realizing just how much my sister and I did suck all the best of her years out of her, but I've learned, painfully, that this is the price we must pay to fight the power. We must fight all the power. Not only the power that's on the right side, in the third drawer from the top. No. *All* the power.

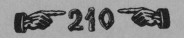

"If you will sssuck my soul,
I will lick your funky emotions
let me kiss your mind./There's nothing wrong with that.
Aaaah, kiss me baby . . . Ow.
I went to New York, got slick, got my hair waves
I was cool . . . heh, heh, I was cool, but I had no groove.
No groove. I had nooo groove. Here it comes,
But now fly on baby, fly on baby, you got it
dig . . . dig . . . dig . . .
fly on sisters, play on brothers . . ."

If you can resist the fornicating waves of these words—even dry, without milk—then I have absolutely nothing more to say to you and we must part ways here so as not to waste any more of each other's time even though we're close to the end of the story of how we saved the citaaay.

As I swerved around the corner, resisting THE MAN and blowing my funky mind, a woman with an afro the size of Venus swaggered down the sidewalk with a bundle under her arm and winked. My trusty hero sidekick, Fishstick, rolled down the window and stuck *out his arm*——POW! POW!—she flew back against the wall with a scream in her throat, a hypodermic needle in her fist, and a bouncing baby bundle in the other.

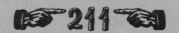

This was a scary place. A bad place. A bad and scary place. It was hell. Ghetto Land, U.S. of A./A place where the atomic pigs would've killed themselves if you'd given them a cold war reprieve and set them free here in Ghetto Land, U.S. oF A. So poor it's like India, and little Sissy's running down the middle of the street and kids are holding their hands out for toilet paper.

Too scary for the swine, but not too scary for the funk. The funky uninsured who flew through life by the seat of their pants. When somebody asked, "Hey, where do you live?" some said, "The Castro." Others answered, "North Beach," or even, "The Mission."

When they asked us, we paused and asked them if they really and truly wanted to know. If they had the courage to go forward with the conversation like one of those Edgar Allan Poe moments where you hear a heartbeat and wanna rip the whole floor up, we went ahead and told them, "We live in a place called Keep-Runnin', California." And when they asked where it was, we said, "It's *waaayy* back . . . way back behind the funk. The raw funk." And they didn't know whether it was the dark space behind the refrigerator or what, but that was just fine with us because either place is dark, scary, and mysterious, with that ubiquitous and dusty low mechanical hum in the background.

Blood spurted up out of our victim's mouth like a water faucet for coloreds only and she writhed on the cement like a bad swimmer while her baby bundle rolled down the front step into a pile of broken crack vials and used condoms floating in a shallow puddle of malt liquor warmed by the noonday sun.

All this pain. Just to live within walking distance of milk, the other white liquid.

"You think this is really gonna work?" Fishstick asked.

I didn't know. You never know. The future of the city was based on my one blow job epiphany in the desert and we could only go forward and apologize later if necessary.

But I believed.

"It's gotta work, damnit." I growled through my teeth and slammed my fists on my funky, low-riding chain steering wheel, and a bead of sweat trickled into the corner of my eye and burned. "It's the only chance our city's got." But I knew he couldn't hear me over the Funkadelic music and

he was going to act too cool to ask me to repeat myself. When you're cool, you never ask anyone to repeat herself because you're so cool, you don't care. Everything inside your head is just the hush of white noise and not giving a damn. This is why being cool is boring. Dentist's waiting-office boring.

I sped away screeching the tires, and up at the stop sign, in my rearview mirror I saw the sign that let me know it was all working just right. I was right all along and that was beauty enough for me, it was worth everything, it was worth wearing the UPS-brown muumuu of oblivion, for in the rearview mirror of our success, I spotted the terror-stricken visage of a Realtor scrambling to get back into her Lincoln Navigator with a teeny silver Wrigley's spearmint gum of a phone stuck to her cheek as she called the police—because by then the cell phones were even *smaller*—while her client fumbled to tear open the door on the passenger's side because he'd changed his mind about buying into our little neighborhood of Keep-Runnin', California, and so they tucked their SUV between their legs and ran away.

But it was a wasted phone call; the coppers don't come 'round here to Keep-Runnin', California. Everyone knew that. It was so bad here, someone could dance around with

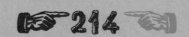

a head on a stick, mock you, and sing, "Go *ahead*, and dial out! La la la!"

We were doing a good job.

In a lovely place like San Francisco, where the air isn't all poison, the sun won't absolutely kill you, and there isn't only iceberg lettuce with green goddess dressing, all you can do is mess with everyone's perception of all the rising property values, low crime rates, good schools, and gays being adorable enough for the afternoon. Like putting a few cops on the corner so everyone thinks crime is down, it's all about perception. We had to screw with people's perception of the city. Once we figured that out, we had our work cut out for us.

Working backward on our list, we'd start off with the Sodomy Porn Coat. We'd be shoving what it really meant to be gay right in their faces. Why? Because you see, not so very long ago, there was a time when someone met a person who was gay and all we could think of as we shook his hand was him getting sodomized. Half the people in my family are gay, and as a child I believed that as soon as I turned my head back real fast, I'd catch Uncle Robert getting it from behind. It was quite distracting while he was alive. And no, he didn't die of AIDS; he died in a

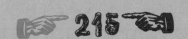

car accident after a bad spat with his lover in a nice restaurant in Vermont where he took the keys and stormed out. That was one dramatic exit his lover will never forget.

But modern versions of Paul Lynde sitcom fags had helped to make gay stuff no longer threatening along with the droning disco beat of Calvin Klein underwear ads at every corner. Superstar lesbians in magazine layouts with their topless girlfriends made lesbianism so fashionable, straight girls flipped coins to sit on each other's laps. Unfortunately we became toothless and had nothing left for anyone to fear as we gummed: *We're here, we're queer, and we're cute as buttons!*

And with everyone settling down with adopted kids or injecting strangers' sperm up their twats, and fighting for gay marriage, the only stark difference between gay and straight life came down to butt-fucking.

So I started sewing porn coats for our people to wear in the streets and while standing in line at Disney movies, wearing my long and flowing quilted sodomy coat with full-color butt-fucking and cock-sucking stills from my favorite boy/boy porn, *Pizza Boy*. It never failed to make some of the new suburban family people cringe and warble,

"Oh for heaven's sake!", nearly poking their children's eyes out with little Boy Scout brooches.

They fear child molesters and beaver shots on the Internet? That's nothing compared to the grotesque real-life spooging fashion of *moi*.

We're here and we're queer? No more. We're here and we're sodomizers and cocksuckers who swallow. Wanna see? Look at the strings in my mouth. Like drinking milk, the other white liquid. I tried to make us as offensive as possible in all ways.

We tried a lesbian sex coat, but lesbian sex only turns people on. We often arrived home with wet spots on our backsides from dads discreetly humping us in the Disney movie line.

And if the Sodomy Porn Coat campaign didn't scare enough of them, we'd remind suburbanites of what they'd feared about the city in the first place: the possibility of having to say "hello" to a passing neighbor if you couldn't make it to your front door fast enough.

But that was greasy kids' stuff compared to what we really had to plan for: we wanted to create a moat of bad and

scary people around the last two ungentrified blocks in San Francisco, a superfund site that coincidentally happened to be a poor black area with a sewage treatment plant. The smell of farts wafted through the air. A bunch of companies further spooged on the masses by having the apartment buildings built on hinges so they could flip them up like trash can lids, to quickly dump more carcinogenic waste underneath them. There is a high rate of breast cancer within those two blocks, but they've got excellent weather and fantastic views of the bay.

A lot more than breast cancer can happen in two blocks. Rats clutched their stomachs and backed out slowly, and it was an unspoken "no fly zone" for pigeons because they dropped dead from all the poisonous gases and fart smells. Jack LaLanne may be out there touting a jumping-jack old age, but he's got the bank account to soften the blow. We didn't care about health. We didn't care about the constant smell of farts permeating the air, or living longer than peasants during the medieval period. Between the social security system and everything else, growing old in America is way overrated, anyhow. You can't even count on getting the high toilet seat.

We were creating our own planned, covenant-controlled community. Like the one Disney did, that creepy little town of Celebration, where they were choking on their own good taste, and flamingoes were the real evil.

But we'd be worse than Disney. We'd create our own scary ghetto version of Disney's small-town community, and instead of cute historic train rides, we'd stage fake drive-by shootings every forty-five minutes to keep the property values down. We'd pay school kids to wander the streets and ask how to spell "cat." We'd pay extra black people to walk around while we played crack addicts and shuffled around with plastic Halloween scabs pasted to our lips like chunky lipstick, acting delirious and offering nightmare blow jobs.

"Fake drive-by shootings?" Fishstick asked. "You mean we point our fingers out of the car and yell 'Bang, bang! You're dead! Now fall down!'?"

No, no, no, I corrected him./We wanted to create fear, or at least that hushed-tone kind of respect lesbians get, because most white folks figured the black ones were always on the verge of rioting anyway—they know that's what they'd do. I know white men who riot if they don't get excellent customer service.

And that's how we ended up with fake blood spurting up out of our phony victim's mouth as she writhed on the cement like a bad swimmer, discreetly adjusting her giant afro wig, while her used Baby Tender Love rolled down the front step into a pile of broken crack vials and unrolled condoms floating in a shallow puddle of malt liquor roasted in the noonday sun.

A pivotal point in our movement was when we got written up in one of the city's two big alternative newsweeklies: *The Cynical Weekly*, which had to be even more cynical than normal, with a jaded staff of thirty-year-olds to make up for the fact that their idealistic paychecks came from one centralized big corporation. And then there was *The Bitter Guardian*, which was particularly whiny about everything, blaming the fall of Rome on anyone who made over ten bucks an hour. Like the dwindling Lesbian Aristocracy, it also had a right to sing the blues, I guess. With only fifteen progressive people left in the city, it was losing readership and was down to printing a handful of cranky newsletters on the Xerox machine, with a single staple in the upper left corner.

From what I remember now, our planned ghetto stunt eventually got covered as one of their rare pieces of hope, where a bunch of artists do performance art, trying to keep their neighborhood to themselves. But the alternative weeklies feel they have to be rebellious and dump on everything regardless of what it is, just for the sake of rebelling. They figure that if you're homeless, you should *be* so homeless, your marrow's even homeless. And if you happen to get a full meal, then you're totally selling out, man.

We were devastated enough at how our bad-ass campaign had suddenly become as "cute" as a sitcom fag, and so when the cynical weeklies did what came naturally to them and made snide fun of us, well let's just say I thought bad thoughts. Very bad thoughts, and whoa! I just—*snapped!*—I could only see the **Blood Red** of their glib newsweekly soy-based inks and I was ready for bear.

But their turning against us turned out to be the least of our worries because once news of our cunning plan came out, there was a big collective "Aaaaw, isn't that cute!" among the yupwazee. It was mere seconds before this was the edgy, hip, industrial chic new place, and on Saturday nights, the cool thing for them to do was to bring a few pints of Courvoisier in the car, wear tight black leather pants from Nordstrom, and prowl slowly into our neighborhood to watch the fake scabby crack whores yell drive-by judgments at them so they could giggle and run back to their cars in mock terror.

Oh, how they laughed and laughed. The boys felt dirty, courageous, and free, like back in the old days when they'd push doorbells and run, run, run away with the wind in their hair. The blond girls did their effeminate parts and dove into the wee, little backseats, squealed like fetal pigs, and tossed their hair back flirtatiously because our chunky, scabby ugliness made them look all that much more fuckable. And that's what Saturday evenings are all about, anyway: looking as fuckworthy as possible in hope of a brighter future.

They felt that even the smell of farts in the air from the sewage treatment plant suddenly gave them the kind of character that Audie Murphy, that war hero/cowboy star, could've only dreamed of. Suddenly they were all power-walking to the neighborhood with cell phones dangling from their ears like coke spoons, calling Realtors, interrupting their *"nam-myoho-rengay-kyo"* chants, and pulling them out of Jacuzzis full of milk.

I'd actually helped to chase the last of affordable San Francisco into an oncoming tidal wave of inattentive Yukon Denali drivers on cell phones crashing through the streets. That was just something I couldn't live with. At least not without trying to blow up something on my way out, first.

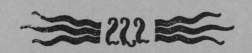

As I sped away from the nail polish remover explosion, proudly looking behind me, I crashed into the wall. Badly. This time I'd finally gone too far. Somehow my spine ended up next to my ear, with my arm casually tossed around my neck like one of those boring pashmina shawls.

I lay there in an extraordinarily uncomfortable position for what seemed like an hour, going over recent events and wondering what exactly I could've done differently.

The sound of footsteps stopped me from mentally slapping my forehead any longer, and I gritted my teeth and tried to cull the magic of Hoochie Mama out of my chocha and into my extremities. But no matter how I concentrated, chanted, and begged, I couldn't move my arms and legs and wondered how that Arabian taxi driver I'd seen in a similar position had gotten out of his little scrape, but I hadn't stuck around to see the ending because I've got this superstition where I figure if I don't look at it, bloody accidents and death won't happen to me.

If I now see any reason to gawk at an accident, it's so you'll know exactly what to do when the same thing happens to you one day.

·2.24·

I heard the footsteps come closer and kick metal out of the way, and through my bent vocal cords and out of *the* corner of my mouth I spit out a molar and burbled the vacant threat, "If you come any closer, I'll stomp you to a flaky-meat pulp after my pulverized legs heal."

Between my inner screams of pain and the torrents of blood racing to the damaged parts of my body to clot and bruise, I couldn't tell whether that was the sound of a giggle I was hearing in the distance or another big, burning piece of metal being shoved out of the way.

Up through the broken window on my side, past the flames, I moved my eyes so far to the corners, the things that held my eyes in my head started to hurt. But no matter . . . I saw a vision of a small woman in a pink muumuu slowly walking through the fire to save me like a fearless Hoochie Mama angel come to save one of her own.

When she reached the door, she stuck her tiny hand through the broken glass to pull the knob up and unlock the door. A line of ice cube diamonds topped the knuckles on her hand, and right before I died, I heard her sniffle and blow her nose.

"Death came + pulled me in like the undertow at the beach. Its power is intoxicating because there's nothing you can do. Little French deaths where porn stars writhe + yell Oooh la la! on your way out of this world. ⊙) * * *

Up through the pine box + The ashes blowing out of the urn, out the open door of the crypt, And from six feet under the worm-eaten, dark, and murky waters that separate the space between the UNDERWORLD + THE UNDERCLASS, I saw a distant light on the surface, getting nearer, like when you look in your rearview mirror + see the headlights of a cop.

★ ★ ★ ★ ★ ★ ★ ★

As I floated there in the dusky waters of in-between, the familiar place I always float before making any kind of tentative move toward heterosexuality or racial identity, I felt a small tug from my belly button, saying, "Okay, okay, it's time to go now." Looking down, I saw a metallic tendril of **THREAD** pulling from my tummy like an umbilical cord, and it shimmered + flashed, up, up and away, into the oncoming headlight, where my dog, Mittens, was barking for me to **COME ON**... come on into the headlight. ～ ARf! ArF! ～

IT FELT SO COUNTERINTUITIVE, BUT MAYBE NOT FOR MITTENS, CONSIDERING HOW SHE DIED. /AND INSTEAD of getting the ANSWERS to LifE, I FINALLY undershood WHY DEER + BUNNIES FROZE BEFORE ONCOMING HEADLIGHTS: They PRObAbLY thought THEY'D **JUST this INSTANt** suddenly DIED, AND that The light WASN'T GOING to THEM, but ThAT **THEY** WERE going iNTO THE LiGht..

YOU CAN CHUCKLE + SAY *isn't that cute* — BUT they're RIGHT as they DO SUDDENLY END UP DEAD, DON'T THEY? You can come at ME with A chicken-or-Egg scenario in EACH Fist + l'll bRUSh YOU away. **HA.** We are young. WHAT DO WE KNOW? PERhaps tiME ISN'T as linear AS WE think. MAybe *Star Trek* is Right. WE LOOK FOR MARTIANS iN OUTER SPACE WHEN OUR OWN INSECT BROTHERS + SISTERS oN THiS PLANET ARE COMPLETE STRANGERS TO US + WE GET SURPRISED THAT BABY LADY BUGS CAN GET SCARED + SCREAM OUT FOR THEIR MOTHERS.
They DO, You KNOW...

... BUT tHERE WAS NO HEADLIGHT FOR ME. ONLY THE Blinding SpOTLIGHT FOR A GAME SHOW with A SMILING HOST IN tHE DISTANCE + Those Podiums YOUR DEAD RELATIVES have to STAND BEhiND... AND Then APPLAUSE AS IT FADES TO COMMERCIAL BECAUSE l Lost *my turn* →

→ life yanked me out from the undertow in the nick of time. Yeah. Just like a mother in a roomy housedress that covers up her soft, little bread-dough stomach. Unless your mother had the audacity to get an unrecognizably flat tummy tuck.

I flashed my eyes open and there I was, I'd made it: once again I was finally the center of everyone's attention, and they were all looking down at me as I lay on the ground. This is what movie stars craved: doting attention without having to suck up to get it.

I looked up at my audience of strange, concerned faces. No matter what was wrong with me, whether I'd crapped Fishstick's pants or would never have the use of my crushed legs again, I wouldn't have wanted it any other way in this moment.

"Tomato—(sniffle)—what in the hell have you been doing?" I heard a woman's voice, punctuated with another blow of the nose. My head was resting on the voice's lap.

I struggled to sit up, unwrap my pashmina arm from around my neck, and look Flower Frankenstein up and down. My car was ablaze behind her and my legs were crushed flat like long soda cans. I remembered thinking, *This is what it'd look like if you actually were stomped by a wooly mammoth.* I must've been in some kind of shock because all I could manage to say over the crackling of the flames was, "What's with the pink muumuu?"

"I wouldn't talk if I were you." She stroked my singed and frizzy hair from my sweaty forehead and tugged at my brown muumuu so it would modestly cover my knees.

"Right after you left, I picked the Hoochie Mama card and became the Mother of the House of Frankenstein."

I found out she took to the muumuu requirement with no problem because she used to live in Hawaii. "Yeah, I've grown up with muumuus. There's the expensive, corporate-gray muumuu you can wear on Fridays; the scoop-neck muumuu, like the one I have on; and the turtleneck Nosferatu muumuu, like the one you're wearing. The flamboyant tourist muumuus come in bright colors and cheap prints, so they're totally white on the other side. The locals wouldn't dare touch such muumuus."

I considered the importance of what she was saying, but wondered, "How did you know I was here? You're magic, aren't you?"

"Yes, not only am I beautiful, but I'm magic." She rolled her eyes and blew her nose. "We actually read about you in the *Cynical Weekly* and I was sent to save you." She glanced over at Fishstick, then back at me. "Well, like what did you guys think you were doing, with all the bombings and stuff, anyway?"

Sheepishly, I looked up at Fishstick and eventually mumbled, "Saving San Francisco."

She looked at the burning shrapnel that crackled on the asphalt all around us and chuckled like a mom. "Saved from whom? This is a damn train wreck, not the work of a woman."

I ignored the latter part. "Saved from whom? Well, look around us." I gestured self-righteously. "The Latte People, of course. They are the train wrecks."

Flower balled up her damp and ragged tissue and dabbed at her nose openings. "Now, where did you get that idea?"

I gawked at her with my mouth open as if she'd dumped a hazelnut frappuccino in my lap. "Look, Flower, this is war. There's no room for this California woo-woo attitude. I want to stay here."

We still didn't hear any sirens. As the flames from the burning car started to singe a nearby tree, I looked around to see if anyone in charge was going to show up and make me go back to jail because of all that I'd done. But everyone was so preoccupied looking for parking and talking on aspirin-sized cell phones that I saw how trying to get a rise out of them was like going up to roadkill, kicking it hard, and saying, "Boy, it's really pissed now!"

"Stay here for what?" Flower asked with a smile.

"We have to take back the city."

"Is that why you're bombing it and stuff?"

"Well, yeah. I was told to start by putting pig heads into Realtors' beds."

"Oh!"—she smacked her forehead and a trickle of wetness popped from her nose. She absently mopped it up with the back of her hand—"That's right. She said she forgot your mission."

"Who?"

"Miss Fabulous, of course. She said her memory's not what it used to be and she lost her train of thought when all the messages were coming through about your future. She figured you'd figure it out once you got here but she didn't know that you'd been in prison before, or why, and so she had no idea you'd be capable of doing all this." Flower spread her arms apart.

"You know her, too?" With all the voices in my head going on diatribes, with all the animated, talking objects, with all the magical strength, and with all the funny dreams, sometimes I wonder if Hoochie Mama and The Pork in the Road at Area 54 in New Mexico was very real at all. She was a one-breasted Amazon woman of our time who, instead of flicking arrows out into the sky, flicked cigarette butts out into the sand. Fishstick was proof that I was even out there. A souvenir from reality. I looked at Fishstick and back at Flower. "You see him, right?"

"Sure."

Nothing surprised me anymore. I just went along without missing a beat. I was cool. White noise cool. No time to stop for questions. Moving right along: "Well, she's the one who gave me the pig head idea."

"I know, I know. She said it was an idea she had for something else. Her mistake."

"Mistake or not, I'm on a mission to save the city."

"I ask you again: save it from what? Look around you, kids. Gentrification happens. You are the SUV driver to the man pushing the shopping cart. Dead people look up at the living with disdain. Someone's always the gentrifier and there's always someone out there who has less."

"But what about the city? It's not silly and fun anymore."

"Look, everyone's getting older. San Francisco is old and tired. Maybe it doesn't even want to be saved. Maybe San Francisco was exhausted of its bawdy history and wants to settle down, slip on some cushy brown vinyl slippers, gulp laxatives out of bottles, wear a smelly striped muumuu, sit back, turn on the TV and tap into a caretaking tax base of rampant twenty-nothings, thirty-nothings, forty-nothings. The overly ambitious who come home after sixty-hour work weeks and trade online just to make the house payments. TINKS.

"Ever think of that? Huh?"

"Tinks. It's a threesome, right?"

"No, it's not about having sex and fun. It's about working. Triple income no kids."

So she explains to me how it's my own opinion of what's good, and how hyper-gentrification's now just a normal progression of our faster lives . . .

". . . Remember the happy-go-lucky days when you were a child and ran around barefoot from sunup to sundown and all you did was play? 'Can you come out and play?'—It wasn't 'Can you come out and do a ten-mile hike?' It was just *go over to a friend's house and _play_*.

"That's all you did from sunup to sundown: 'What do you wanna do?'/'I don't know, what do *you* want to do?'/'I don't know . . .' And you'd see how long you could go through the summer without wearing shoes with the sun at your back. Make bets and see who can go the longest without wearing shoes, ever.

"And that's the way San Francisco was. Everyone was just running around having fun, going barefoot, standing on the corner having a forty, and having sex in the park.

"But now everything's more specific, you can't just call for the hell of it. You've gotta entice someone with an idea. We don't just say, 'Hey, let's go out and stand on the corner with a forty.' Why? Because it's not that much fun anymore.

"Now everyone's got a job, and they've all gotta support that *Leave It to Beaver* environment that was shoehorned into our lives when we were little. We've been brainwashed by hours and hours of twenty-four frames per second. The replay button's stuck and we're thinking: 'I'm supposed to have really clean sidewalks, get the Bermuda shorts and mow my lawn, and wave at the neighbors . . .'

"We want the neighborhoods to be safe safe safe, but forget how all that time when we were running around, we'd run around with scissors. We don't run around with scissors anymore.

"We fix the sidewalks and paint all the houses so everything's perfect like *Leave It to Beaver*. But we also forget that it was really about all the fun and trouble that Beaver had. It was about Eddie Haskell getting Beaver to do shit that he shouldn't do.

"And that's how San Francisco *was*. Between all the whores, drugs, sex, music, brawls, and whatever, we sat around and did shit that we shouldn't do. Now that we're grown up we're just looking at the backdrop. We've lost sight of what *Leave It to Beaver* was all about. It's all a big metaphor for what we shouldn't do.

"Soooo"—she clapped her knees in summation—"I guess the final question you have to ask yourself is, Do you want to do what it takes to live in San Francisco? Drive around in a car with a hamburger in your lap, Palm Pilot in one hand, phone to your ear, driving with your knees, running over occasional children on tricycles? Your greatest asset is your time. Your own time, to do with it what you want." She stood up, blew her nose with a fresh tissue, and looked at her watch. "—Ooops! Speaking of which, it's time for us to go. Come on, if you want to join us. We're outa here. We're off like a prom dress."

"Uhm." I nodded toward my legs. "Is the revolution wheelchair accessible, because I'm not exactly—"

"—Oh my goodness!" Her eyes bulged and she pointed over my shoulder. "What's that?"

It was only a distraction, for when I looked back, my legs were full and shiny again. Like long, uncrushed soda cans. As if nothing had ever happened. Eerie. Very eerie.

"Whoa! Something funny's going on around here." Earlier, my floppy carpal tunnel hand had also been instantly HEALed BY ANOTHER woman WEARING A muumuu—Coincidence? Or not?—I suspected much, but without proof, I'd only get as far as the receptionist at *Star Magazine*.

"Oh, piffle. I'll hear of no such thing. Come on." Flower pulled back the cellophane wrap on a new personal-pak of tissues and walked away.

Having nothing left to lose, and nowhere else to go with my own free time now that I'd just wasted even more of it yet again, I got up to follow her, leaving my toys on the front lawn and my car burning in the background, like a child called in for the night. Everything would be covered with dew in the morning.

But Fishstick just stood behind, with his hands on his hips and a pained look on his face.

"What's wrong? C'mon, let's go." I sheepishly motioned for my faithful sidekick to follow.

"What she said sounds good. I think that I want to be a grown-up. I'm ready to do what it takes to live in San Francisco."

So here it was; it's all in how you decide to look at it. Another moment that reminds you how weird it feels to be the last one at the rickety kids' table. Yet another childhood friend lost to a marriage, a child, a real job, a boring grown-up's city.

All along, Fishstick had been sort of a reluctant superhero sidekick. He stuck around helping me out with my superhero duties hoping that I'd eventually complete the blow job I started back on the bridge that day, but I never did. After I got his pants, he didn't have anything else I wanted. And whenever I felt the need for the instant, clamoring praise that the ability to perform fellatio will bring, I simply reached for a gun and stroked the dark blue barrel of a .38, and the need went away.

So it was no real surprise that the day had come when he'd tell me that he wanted to stay behind and find someone special to finish the life-affirming blow job I'd begun. A blow job that had spurred him onward to a new life in a new world. Ah, a hard act to follow. Maybe he'll find a new little smiling girl in a pair of summery white capris, carrying a corporate coffee cup. Someone to lay eggs with, and raise larvae.

He explained, "I'm like a Vulcan heeding the mating call." Already knee-deep in animal and *Star Trek* metaphors, he goes on to explain how it's like a salmon swimming upstream. He's got to do it and, yeah, eventually he wants a garage, a car, a driveway, and a yard. He'll want things to be a little more horizontal, but he wants to make a killing. And for the first time I really listened to who he was. *He* was one of those people who came to the city, not to be himself—in blue hair or to fuck other boys—but to make a million dollars and send around stupid joke e-mails. No matter how good I was at giving head, I could never make the erection for all this **GO AWAY.** Good thing I hadn't even tried, and Lord help the woman who thinks she can.

I had to accept his choice for happiness as nicely as if he'd just come out to me as a Puerto Rican transgendered Muslim homosexual. Why? Because if this city's taught me anything, it's taught me tolerance.

—Can you hear the national anthem? I can.

I swallowed hard past the goiter of sadness in my throat, clapped him on the shoulder through the national anthem, and said, "I hear you, my son." And now that I was tolerant, I hugged him for who he really was: a straight white boy into Internet humor who used *Star Trek* references to explain his sexual needs.

And wasn't it only natural for him to feel at home amongst the other boys bathed in the romantic blue lights of their computers? I was speechless until I felt his perpetual teepee under those boxer shorts of his. "Hey, Mister Happy Pants, go and get rid of that kickstand of yours before you make some kind of mistake." I lovingly punched him on the arm, laughed with a good-bye tear in my eye. "Now I know they also call you 'Fishstick' because that little thumb of yours is always sticking out, looking for a ride."

He had a big tear in his eye, too. "Yes. Now you know the truth, but I guess it doesn't matter because we'll never see each other again.

"When I was fourteen, my 'dad said it was time to show me what love was all about. He said *let's go to a whorehouse in Elko, Nevada.* Ever since that day, I don't

think I've been soft for longer than ten minutes. They thought it was some kind of calcification problem. I couldn't even stand up in church.

"My girlfriend thought it was great. But after the first six hours, it wasn't conceptual anymore. Said she didn't wanna get all raw and bloody, so I've been having sex with warmed-up zucchini skins since then." He sniffled tears back and clapped his face into his hands. "That was the best blow job I'd ever had."

"Yes, yes, I know." And I did know, so I hugged him once more, patting him on the back. "Well, tiger, you'll always have your memories." But I also knew that there should come a day when he'd grow up, look out the window, take a sip of coffee and realize that it really wasn't *that* great after all. I wiped my nose with the back of my hand as I kicked a gum wrapper back and forth with my toe.

241

"Thank you, I will."

"And God willing that you don't get Alzheimer's from eating pork with aluminum forks, you'll always be thankful for being able to look back on it like a porn-memory flash card. That's how I learned the alphabet and all my lessons in life." I reached into the pocket where I'd slushed his

suicide note, and I handed it back to him. "Here, I never even read it. I don't need it."

"Yes, yes you do." He cupped his hands over my outstretched hand. "It'll be a little something to remember me by." Out of the mouths of sidekicks.

"Aw, go put some pants on, you little rascal, and quit your lollygagging." I swatted his butt like a horse in those cowboy movies where the horse runs away and the one on the horse gets hanged from the tree.

Watching him turn AROUND and RUN into the never-rich-enough, never-thin-enough arms of San Francisco's future, I glanced at the note in my hand and walked over to the trash can and let it go, along with all of my own expectations.

I trotted to catch up with Flower Frankenstein and the others, but stopped in my tracks: "Did it say . . . ?— Nah . . ." And I started to leave again. But was that a drawing of a slice of bacon I saw? And in the same unsure way I first met and misunderstood Fishstick, I turned around and returned to the trash can to be sure, absolutely sure, because this was the kind of life where everything was a sign. With all the clamoring out there, I just need to be careful that it's not only more pictures of soda spliced into the film to make me thirsty.

Angling my arm down into the trash can was so disgusting, I almost walked away without retrieving the strangest thing this Hoochie Mama ever found. Maybe it's nothing. Maybe it was nothing then, maybe it's still nothing now. Maybe it's only me, but it doesn't matter because even the paranoid have enemies and buttered bread has a 50 percent chance of falling butter-side down.

The point is, some of us are lucky enough to be receiving little e-mail messages from God himself, while the rest of us are stumbling around the forest looking for magic in the signs we see, about what to do next so we've got at least a sliver of a chance at being right: a vague Bazooka Joe fortune, a lightbulb flickering, a car starting up, a cosmic nod of the universe's head that it's all going to be okay. I didn't need anything more, like a dog named Mittens, I didn't need a pack of tarot cards, I didn't need a rabbit's foot, big tits or a pretty face to get me by.

Even if we were wrong, bad things are often good in the end, like getting fat, or like that big facial scar that finally forces you to be an interesting person. You've got to face the g-force of the future with that belief if you're to have hope. I guess it's all in how you wanna look at things—whether that glass is empty, full, or has jagged edges—I suppose there is no answer, no right or wrong thing. Even my mom remembers that time we got evicted in West Virginia as motivation to get her own house so no one could ever do that again.

Anyhow, the day I pulled the note out of the trash, I blotted the coffee off the corner, unfolded it. It'd been torn from a spiral notebook, and I lovingly evened some of the tattered edge up, squinted my eyes and focused on the paper bacon scars from where he'd ripped the pinned note off his chest.

At first it looked like nothing more than a grocery list. But that's what it wanted you to see, because when I looked at the paper again, closely, it said things. As the coffee spot evaporated into beige, neatly written capital letters said:

"Don't wash, Josephine, I'm coming home . . ."

I recognized it as Jack LaLanne's handwriting, but I knew it was what Napoleon supposedly wrote in a love letter to Josephine so he could find his way home by the smell of her French crotch alone.

That's about as good as the magic note ever got. As with children, the Internet, and my good intentions, the magic note started out with a bang, but quickly settled deep into the large intestine of mediocrity. The magic note could've used its power to grant monkey-paw wishes or tell me the future. Instead, it usually gave me the same stupid e-mail jokes I'd already deleted way back in Netscape 2.0.

And so I must also admit here and now that I didn't really save any city. It didn't take me long to see that the magic letter's allusion to Napoleon and his thing for *petite* French crotch smells was the magic letter's way of making fun of me and my botched attempt to save San Francisco. With both of us, our good intentions turned out to be more like spraying FDS in a whorehouse so no one would know./Especially if Josephine was lurking about with three wavy lines between her legs.

I guess this is precisely what Flower Frankenstein meant when she said that I must be careful, because if I got out of balance, I'd be allowing selfishness to rule. That "no matter how noble your original intent, secret fears and worries will cast despondent shadows over the brightest events."

Rats. Foiled again. I knew that I'd figure it all out once it was too late. This is why I go around, snorting and sniffing for the right advice like Napoleon, that wacky truffle pig. Unless you stick to something like the Bible and find an interpretation you can stomach, it's difficult to make it all up as you go along and do the right thing. It's so hard to live for any cause you think is noble without turning into a complete asshole somewhere along the process, and alienating the whole world—even your own mother.

But we've all been under a lot of stress. None of us have really been the same ever since the computer programmers, delirious with Silicon Valley's kisses, came to dinner and peed all over the toilet seat out of excitement. And fifty years after the GI bill that started the whole suburban, distant-milk thing, the Russians are busy playing Cowboys and Indians while the Japanese are setting their endangered species pets free for Lent, apologizing for greed and finding God now that the economy's bad and they've got a minute. Presently, our own neurotic baby boomers are collecting homes and parcels of land like baseball cards and frantically jamming shoe boxes of deeds under their Swedish beds.

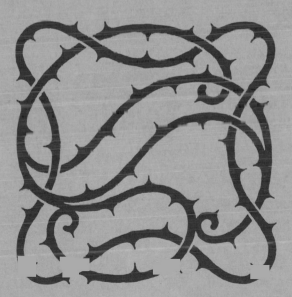

My Dream Shoes

ow that I'm older, I'm gonna have to go to Target—even though it's bad—and finally get a box of ninety-six crayons to see for myself what happened with the pink-pig "flesh" crayon controversy. My days of having three crayons are over.

Everything used to be in threes: three wishes, three strikes, three acts. But it looks like seven is really the lucky number. We can only really keep track of seven good friends at a time in our lives; and then of course there are seven deadly sins; seven basic Shakespeare plots; seven seas; seven horsemen of the apocalypse; seven days of the week; the seventh seal; and 7-Eleven—which is now open 24-7 because everything's open all the time.

When you get to "eight," it all goes downhill and that's when the guessing begins. Seven's the tipping point, and we wanted to leave the land of eight-digit salaries and nine-digit rents, to go back to a time when tiny local phone numbers were only seven numbers long and you didn't need extra note paper or a Palm Pilot just to write down the area code for the next street over, a time when 7-Eleven was actually open from seven to eleven, back when we didn't have pagers and answering machines. Phones had busy signals and it was a world where you

could always call back later. A world where there was a LATER. A land where people with hair in their cracks served you anything but apple pie, because in Amerika with a "k," it's not at all about mom and apple pie.

We'd made the silly mistake of believing our own urban-bohemian hype and thought: "I live in San Francisco; therefore I'm creative." As if just living here would make us creative bohemians. But it was time to stop riding bitch on the patchouli coattails of others' bohemian histories and make our own.

Why are we really holding on to this town? Is this town an accessory? Can't we be bohemians where it's cheaper? Why do we have to make it so hard on ourselves in the city with the bohemian thing? And why stay in a place where all the cool people are gone, anyway?

We forgot it wasn't about *where* we lived, but about having time and space to make stuff and enjoy ourselves. Living in the city stopped being about art and was about lifestyle. Being a bohemian has become an accessory, like punk rock collectibles on e-Bay and people who have dogs like handbags. To buy style instead of do it, create it, live it. Sure, it's easier because everything's collectible now. Even the disco memories of sitting like a board because you were so smushed into your designer jeans they moved your liver and left permanent seam lines on your skin. They are more valuable now than they were the first time because crushing your burning pussy with denim seams actually *sucked*. We did the punk thing, and now it's like an old avocado refrigerator color phase because they were pure for a short time.

We should also stop pressing our noses against the sliding glass doors of 7000 square-foot homes, watching the Jones's sit around their redwood Christmas tree and unwrap the latest translucent Macintosh.

Andy Warhol wrote that the best time to go to the park in the city is when it's raining because you have it all to yourself. So I agree that it's high time we bought up what's left of the old suburban lifestyle at Goodwill, scrape off someone's old snot, and pretty it up with a dab of spit and polish. As long as we didn't take our lawns too seriously, it'd work just fine for us the second time around.

But this time let's keep our addresses a secret, before trailer parks and aluminum siding become all the rage, like those jackets with the embroidered first names on them. Maybe we'll have a committee take away the street signs so no one knows how to reach us and we'll give outsiders the

evil eye. I have faith that in time other underachievers will eventually find us, like beads of mercury. We'll ignore the fact that we could become a creepy inbred community, and deal with that later like the Israelis.

And so like the witnesses of the last days of Pompeii, we grabbed our crayons and ran, ran, ran as fast as we could, out of San Francisco and away from the Silicon Valley Latte People, frantically tearing across the bridge for our lives like the chick in the woods in those slasher horror movies. Our tits bounced and our mascara streamed down our cheeks. No one would take away our milk money again. Ever again. All you could see was a scribble of people in different colors on their way to another promised land of cheap rent and enough free time to have sex and to sleep, perchance to dream those existential anxiety dreams we were intended to have.

We ran, ran, ran, and ran into the last of the sex-havers who were still having intercourse with their legs up in the air and ankles clipped behind their ears like change purses, even as they ran across the Golden Gate Bridge. It was even more amazing than men having sex together in those locker rooms.

In shiny new gold carpal tunnel braces, the UPS drivers gulped down handfuls of herpes medicine, clapped the sex-havers on the back as they passed, then tearfully waved good-bye to the rest of us like the men with the golden arms in our nightmares. We wandered away from the city and out into the desert of parking spaces and tract homes. The money blowing all around us thinned to the occasional grimy penny glued to the ground with urine and spit.

"Ninety-six crayons of color on the WALL
ninety-six crayons of color,
break the crayon, la la la,
and you've got ninety-five crayons of color on the wall."

Oh, how we sang our little embroidered-nametag hearts out as we wandered away from the beige, and scribbled furiously over the atomic tangerine lines, past the purple pizzazz page, and skipped off into the melted crayon pink carrot, macaroni n' cheese, and neon lobster butt sunset.

Miraculously, I still have all my teeth, which is a good thing because once in a while I need to chew on my fried eggs to soften them up for later. My cooking's not what it used to be, but no matter—the revolution's not supposed to taste good. I quickly write these words to you in the blackest hours of the night, clutching a flashlight between my teeth under the bed covers.

Even though a few of us escaped and are relatively safe as of this moment, I look around me with binoculars at all the mice-crushing Latte People and *I am still afraid.* Very, very afraid. Afraid of the oblivious ones who never, ever mean to crush the mouse, but whenever they're around, someone's always got to die, move out, take a pay cut, or go without milk. I can try and open my heart up to the lighter side of the Latte People, but it always leads to . . . *dead mice.*

I tell you this whole story to let you know that I've seen fear, I know fear. I've been its mistress, its butt boy, its lover, its wife, its servant, its beastmaster. I've seen the monkey paw wishes for prosperity turn into uninsured, ghetto-emergency-room terror.

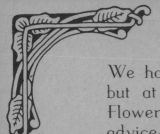

We had our ideas that things could get even more ironic, but at the time we weren't totally sure how. Between Flower's cards, my magic suicide letter, the wise, advice-giving knot above my ankle, and tyromancy (divining by the coagulation of cheese), we were still flying by the hems of our muumuus into the not quite certain, crayon-colored future. Maybe your pussy lips steered you right in the desert once, and maybe your horoscope was right last week, but it's hard to know who or what to listen to on a regular basis for advice.

Regardless of what magic we were privy to, unlike those who formed rigid political opinions by watching the new *Saturday Night Live* and propping their platform shoes up on coffee tables made out of homeless peoples' teeth, we couldn't relive the seventies or eighties all over again, in the hopes of doing the last decades over without being surprised this time.

All we knew for absolute sure was the power of the muumuu as long as we were wearing it, and that there was no Mothers Against Drunk Drivers for people like us. Loafers = Death, and it's a No Chinos environment. We were the National Association for the Advancement of the Crayon People with robin's-egg blue laughter, sex the color of sunglow and wild watermelon, and freedom the color of

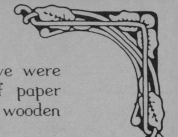

razzle-dazzle rose and Granny Smith apples, and we were gonna write it all down on a long, long roll of paper hanging by the side of our new kitchen phone in a wooden notepad shaped like an old-fashioned sled.

So here it is. In your hands you hold evidence of the only selfless act I've ever committed in my entire life. You must consider this story as a warning. A warning before it's too late, because they *all* want your apartment in that funky neighborhood where it's within convenient proximity of milk, the other white liquid. And they're willing to whisper "$40,000 over the asking price" in your landlord's hot and sweaty ear, and throw in a cruise to Disneyland. This is the banality of JUST PETTIN' IT GEORGE/LATTE PEOPLE evil, where we try to make a ton of excuses to a lumbering higher power named Lenny.

If you don't believe what I say, I'll ask if you remember when they found out that the big black Martian book, *To Serve Man*, was not about doing favors for Man, like bringing Man the evening paper and slippers, but a cookbook on how to serve Man *as* supper . . .

If you don't remember that cookbook fiasco, well, there was a whole lot of hush-hush along with the atomic pigs. We're all gonna pay. Oh boy, are we gonna pay. Some of us think that we die and that's it. Karmic debt. I can't even toss gum out of a car window without stepping on it five hundred miles later that day. Oh yes. Explain that, cranky cynics who haven't seen heaven except in their own pierced belly buttons.

Andrew Carnegie's probably already come back a few times over as one of Hugh Hefner's personal-use Playboy Bunnies with good ol' Hugh's ancient mothball essence running down her legs because he detests condoms; while Bill Gates will come back as a retarded crayfish in one of those streams he's contaminated from monthly computer obsolescence. A crayfish who dreams of being a big Hollywood star, but can't stay out of the water long enough to even ride one of those special buses to school.

Then let's see a future reincarnation episode of *Where Are They Now?* on the Has-Been Channel, so the meek who inherit the earth can fill their chemotherapy days with cancer-riddled pleasure and gloat while coughing up whatever dust the radiation kicks up at the oncological hoedown. These future children will be called Phlegm Bunnies, and you've just gotta love 'em because they haven't done a damn thing wrong.

Anyway, it's too late for San Francisco, but not for you. There isn't much time, so you'd better get started. Take my word for it, there are rotting monsters under YOUR bed, with worms tumbling out of their eyesockets, too. Worms that open those same miniature worm mouths and cry for REVENGE! shriek for JUSTICE! and caterwaul for your scalp. Don't look to your mom for help—or even your grandma—because not only are they wearing mental muumuus, rolling their eyes, wondering when you'll finally leave them alone, but times are different now. The waiting list for trailer parks may be long and Jack LaLanne may be cool again, but it's up to you to eat right and do the kegel exercises to keep the recliner dry.

If I weren't still wearing this magic muumuu and therefore too tired to even get up, I'd do it myself, but you'll have to be the ones who swallow the fear and the courage, along with the robustness of choice and sometimes dizzying consequences. And be sure and bring me a piece of chicken when you're done. Forget the white meat and just bring me the skin. I'm trying to watch my churlish figure.

Speaking of long-lost girlish figures: at the end of that Caroline Kennedy swollen-ankle summer, I also finally realized that the sound of something corpse-heavy and dull being slowly dragged back and forth throughout the decades of my nightmares actually wasn't the body of my childhood puppy, Mittens. No. But my once comforting explanation turned out to be something even scarier . . .

. . . It really *was* a bag of flour being schlepped across the floor . . . but it was for the bloodcurdling lingonberry biscotti all along.

TAKE A CHANCE ON

Euro Evil .

It seemed like the Latte People had won, until the day they looked around the city and found that they were surrounded by all the neighbors they went to high school with back in the 'burbs. You closed your eyes and couldn't hear the Ebonics anymore: not only the city, but entire societies of people had become gentrified like Bryant Gumble.

Without Mexican men to move their furniture, or black people to make them nervous; without gay boys to teach them style, or lesbians to feel self-righteous indignation for them; and without beggars to make them feel generous, or thieves to remind them to be grateful, San Francisco turned into a city full of boring white people with no rhythm. A little Europe.

It was only a matter of hours before Brooks Brothers catalogues filled every mailbox and people sent foil-covered cheeses for Christmas. It was only a matter of minutes before they stopped sharing their feelings and started blaming global warming on welfare recipients. And it was only a matter of seconds before that Euro techno disco filled the streets and Abba became really, really big again. I mean *huge*.

And like prostitution and marriage, the tradition of noblesse oblige is a long one that's tried and true. It's about the natural balance of things because the rich know they need the poor around in order to not only be rich, but to simply *feel* rich. In modern total disregard for this historical balance, criminals could no longer afford to live in San Francisco. As a result, some of the Latte People snapped and turned to crime in a desperate attempt to make the city interesting again.

HONDO Flammers himself turned to crime out of need. There was no end to renovating his collection of old and charming Victorians, and when he lost thousands of dollars on the "unexpected" Amazon.com crash, he took to wearing a ski mask and holding up Home Depot for crown molding and pedestal sinks. After spending all the thousands of dollars he'd made in the stock market at Home Depot, of course the staff knew every mole and wrinkle on his body, so even with a ski mask the puzzled cashier held his hands up and asked, "Mr. HONDO? Is, is that you?" And of course HONDO could only try and disguise his voice and answer, "No! No! It's not me!"

And if irony's in the details, you can't usually pick through the box of linty details until you're safely sprawled out on a sofa, watching Jack LaLanne exercise on TV. Maybe he's a martian; he barely breaks a sweat. The jumpsuits alone are as mesmerizing as penises with fins, or magazine promises of a better way, but it's his promise of getting old without having to crap your pants on the shag carpeting that makes me want to wrap my arms around his neck and ride around the house piggyback.

And so now I can tell you it's true when they say the best revenge is living well, because there we were in the linty suburbs, where there was a washer and dryer for every boy and every girl. After wandering forty days and forty nights, oh my, how we needed them. Good night!

A little sky-blue latex, a few close-out gallons of high-gloss pork pink for the trim, and it'd all shine up just fine. The geek may inherit the earth, but we'd inherit the suburbs and hang out in the flaking kidney-shaped swimming pools like big shots. In the moonlight, chips of paint floating on the surface look like water lilies.

And so there we were, changing the channel of life because we didn't like what was on, and living *la vida Beaver* like the first housewives after the war, always keeping our tower of martini glasses overflowingly full. We were actually keeping in touch and dropping by, having barbecues at our tastelessly painted 2000 square-foot suburban tract homes and swimming in our murky backyard pools. And once again, we looked like we were having such a damn good time, all the Latte People wanted back into the houses they'd abandoned for MORE, on their way to HAVING IT ALL, and getting it NOW.

Funny thing was that by the time they realized that our own oscar-brown grass was still way more interesting, the economy had turned, and it was too late: there was a sweaty hush across the wires as the Latte People suddenly stopped buying limited edition VW Beetles over the Internet. Tattered Neiman Marcus bags blew in the wind and abandoned Range Rovers cluttered the sides of the highway. They couldn't unload their $1.5 billion 500-square-foot faux lofts and come back to the swimming pools we were peeing in.

HA, HA, THAT'S SO FUNNY, EVEN AUNT DAD REMEMBERED TO LAUGH.

Thanks to MARK Ramsey, of RAMSEY PROPERTIES, for renting me this APARTMENT when I didn't even HAVE a job yet... Thanks to MY SISTER FOR helping ME to Focus MY SEETHING ANGER + fear into this FANTASY: "You're my favorite sister... I know, I know... MY ONLY SISTER." Thanks again to MARY "CHERRY" STARVLS for being like A FINISHING School for me, so I bring wine to dinner and wipe my feet off AT THE DOOR. THANKS for TEACHING ME BALANCE and Now I do Dishes + straighten up after "myself." / AND FLOWER FRANKENSTEIN for her génerosity + WISDOM + all of her Bikini Kat® DRAWINGS in here / JEFFREy HICKEN, MY HARLEY-RIDING MAN-FRIEND WHO GIVES me FUNNY IDEAS + FURRY FISH + GOOD TASTE. He fell IN Love with A JERSEy girl because That's WHAT you DO with them. Her name's vicky + she HAS a Harley, too.

(and it was someone like Jeffrey's great-grandfather who "discovered" this particular fur-bearing trout on page 196)

*"DISCOVER" like the G-SPOT and AMERICA...

THANKS to KRIS KOVICK for bringing ME out to San Francisco + giving me a place to stay in the middle of her Bone cancer six years ago. /Now she's a scary-scary landlady. BEING INAPPROPRIATE

...and thanks to MY FRIENDS FOR Listening to Me PRATTLE on + ON About gentrification + A homeless future...

Emily + Alex / Mary, again / My whole address book...

AND a special Place in my heart + My PANTS for James Swanson, MY GUY. FRIEND who likes the kind of sports where he gets ROCKS stuck in his knees and blood trickling down his BACK... MAN-stuff.

AND in New York, the city that — COMPARED to Madrid — is in A downRight COMA... I'd like to THANK Editor CHUCK ADAMS FOR TAKING ME ON... DAVID ROSENTHAL, the Big muckety-muck over there at Simon + Schuster. Mrs. CHERYL WEINSTEIN... AND then "MR. AMAZO"

...Jim Thiel, the production guy who insists he's just a cog in the wheel + makes no decisions. He said if robbers broke in his house they'd say, "Hey, I threw that out last year." / Thanks also to PRODUCTION EDITOR, TED LANDRY, and his BAND of PERFECTIONISTS: Maria Massey; James Swanson; and Tia Maggini...

... MY ART FRIEND, PAUL SMITH... Law MAN, M.J. Bogatin, FOR PEACE OF MIND...

ALONG with my 9th grade English teacher, Della Williams, I'd like to include secret agent Leigh Feldman + my old editor, Big Daddy Bob, EVEN though WE NO longer work together, because they helped ME SOOO much ♥...

Thanks to Sharon Gibbons FOR "trying" to be my editor: Good luck, wherever you are. / THANKS to MARK LAMMERS FOR his OFFICE + PUMPKIN PIE...

..AND LET'S THANK KRIS KOVICK again FOR TELLING ME TO WRITE about MEAT THE WAY I do that Other stuff: "SHOW A little PINK."

AND THANK You all FOR Your encouraging letters... MAY You all always have SUNNY APARTMENTS!